THE
LOS ANGELES
REVIEW

THE — LOS ANGELES REVIEW

VOLUME 21 • SPRING 2017

EDITOR • KATE GALE

GUEST EDITOR • MELANIE JEFFREY

MANAGING EDITORS • REBECCA BAUMANN & KEATON MADDOX

FICTION EDITORS • ALISA TRAGER & MEREDITH ALDER

POETRY EDITORS • BLAS FALCONER & VANDANA KHANNA

NONFICTION EDITOR • ANN BEMAN

ASSISTANT NONFICTION EDITOR • FLORENCIA RAMIREZ

TRANSLATION EDITOR • PIOTR FLORCZYK

BOOK REVIEWS EDITOR • ALYSE BENSEL

ASSISTANT BOOK REVIEWS EDITOR • DANIEL PECCHENINO

CONTRIBUTING EDITOR • TOBI HARPER

COPY EDITOR • REBA NUTTING

PUBLISHER • SELENA TRAGER

THE LOS ANGELES REVIEW IS A PUBLICATION OF RED HEN PRESS

The Los Angeles Review (ISSN 1543-3536) is published by Red Hen Press.
Copyright © 2017 by Red Hen Press

The Los Angeles Review is published annually. The editors welcome electronic submissions of fiction, nonfiction, poetry, book reviews, profiles, and interviews. Please go to www.losangelesreview.org for guidelines and reading periods. All rights revert to author on publication.

Subscription rates for individuals: US $20.00 per year. Libraries and institutions: $24.00 per year. Subscriptions outside the US add $10.00 per year for air mail. Classroom and bookstore discounts available. Remittance to be made by money order or by a check drawn on a US bank.

Visit us online at www.losangelesreview.org.

Cover design by Alicia Kleman

ISBN: 978-1-59709-485-6

Acknowledgments: The works and ideas published in *The Los Angeles Review* belong to the individuals to whom such works and ideas are attributed, and do not necessarily represent or express the opinions of Red Hen Press, any of its advisors or other individuals associated with the publication of this journal. Certain works herein have been previously published and are reprinted by permission of the author and/or publisher.

The National Endowment for the Arts, the Los Angeles County Arts Commission, the Dwight Stuart Youth Fund, the Max Factor Family Foundation, the Pasadena Tournament of Roses Foundation, the Pasadena Arts & Culture Commission and the City of Pasadena Cultural Affairs Division, the City of Los Angeles Department of Cultural Affairs, the Audrey & Sydney Irmas Charitable Foundation, Sony Pictures Entertainment, Amazon Literary Partnership, and the Sherwood Foundation partially support Red Hen Press.

CONTENTS

NONFICTION

TRANSLATIONS

REVIEWS

TO OUR READERS

KATE GALE

In what world would we not need stories? Perhaps there was a country, a city, a valley, a place, where people were at peace, where all kinds of people however different, sat down together to break bread, to play music, perhaps then, stories didn't call and buzz and itch to be told. But if there was such a time, it is not now.

We storytellers wake up in the middle of the night, we wake early, we write late into the moments when the curve of the moon melts the horizon and still we write to wake the dead, to arouse the living into action. A year of police killings of African Americans, of violence in Paris, Istanbul, and Aleppo and then this divisive election that made so many of us question our fellow citizens. What country do we live in? What story do we inhabit?

More than ever now, we need writers. We need writers like Laurie Ann Doyle who writes in "Just Ask for Hateman," "A Hate Camp sprung up in the park," and that sums up America at the end of 2016. A hate camp sprang up in the park, in the neighborhood, in the lines between red and blue. More than ever, we need to write, to think, and to reach out to each other. We live in an age where it's easy to make assumptions, to post our own truth to social media, but it's our job as writers to discover someone else's story. We need to listen, read, think, write. I invite you to dig in to a place for thinkers—this issue of *The Los Angeles Review*. In it, Lauren K. Alleyne writes:

"Here is the night snarled with starts, here is the smile / full of teeth. . . . / Here is naked. Here, light by an exploring moon. . . . / Here is the old road you have longed and longed to travel / It hisses your name. . . . / There is no turning here; here you learn how to burn."

AFAA MICHAEL WEAVER

A POSTSCRIPT TO GIANT

"A Postscript to Giant" and "Making Soldiers" are part of the author's new book of poems, *Spirit Boxing*, in the Pitt Poetry Series from U Pitt.

In the backseat of that yellow Buick he bought
working at the cotton mill, at the Drive-In
under the full moon, her mama and daddy gone
down to Macon to see Aunt Sally, nothing
to hold them back from pulling at each other
until before the moon could say how sprite it was
they were pulled on top of each other, flipping
open the door to consequences. He been working
twice as hard ever since. That movie was *Giant*,
don't they remember? Every time he asks her,
they get older in the gray hobbling along, alone.

Down by that creek on his daddy's first place
there was a frog that used to croak out like it knew
what would happen if he messed with her. Kiss Clara,
won't nothing ever be clear again, pull on her lips
as long as you want you'll be pulling lines to move
long rails of steel in place on construction sites,
worlds for other men, filling their bank accounts.

The frog croaked to dumb ears
when they eased into each other, forgetting all about
James Dean covered with black crude trying to seduce
the one beauty, Elizabeth Taylor, while the beauty
of a naked innocence dies, a debt sealed by paper.

Afaa Michael Weaver

Making Soldiers

The drill sergeant loved asses and elbows,
the only things he wanted to see, summary
of being busy at what we were told to do,
crawling one hundred yards on flat belly.

Our elbows alligator feet with icky webs,
our own feet the twisted fins of prehistoric
fish still undiscovered, or maybe living
still in the place where we were going,

some jungle, some desert, some mountain
on the other side of New Jersey, the state
with gorgeous elbows. If you ever doubt,
just turn the map sideways to find the arms

of millions of people jutted out to show
elbows to be in fact the half ass of the arm
made whole only when the arms are pulled
together with palms up in hasty prayer.

In the swirl of doing the funky chicken,
a sexy comfort food for hungry alligators,
we stood at the edge of fields to learn
how to grow rough leather skin, to kill

inside the heart, with a treacherous smile.

GUEST EDITOR

MELANIE JEFFREY

GUEST

EDI

TOR

GUEST EDITOR

MELANIE JEFFREY

I FIRST HEARD LAUREN K. ALLEYNE'S poetry at the Poetry Circus, an annual event held in front of the carousel at Griffith Park in Los Angeles. As she read her poem, I was taken by the smooth cadence and imagery of "Love in B minor":

Your sandbag body. Your blank moon eyes.

Your glasses a train derailed across your nose.

Your legs folding like bendable straws.

I immediately bought her book and sheepishly asked for an autograph because I'm a poet, and other poets are my rockstars.

When asked to be a guest editor for *The Los Angeles Review*, I knew that I wanted to talk to Alleyne about her poetry. Currently, Alleyne is the Assistant Director of the Furious Flower Poetry Center at James Madison University in Virginia. We conducted our interview via telephone and Google Docs. I called her on a Sunday morning in August. She currently is trying to live without the internet at home so she can focus on her craft; in order to be online during our interview, she graciously went to a McDonald's.

Jeffrey: I read in your bio that you were born in Trinidad and Tobago; how did you find yourself in Virginia?

Alleyne: I arrived in VA via a winding way, which is in a sense, typical for academia: you go where the job is! I recently (two days ago to be precise) began a new position as the Assistant Director of The Furious Flower Poetry Center at James Madison University, and so I'm now a proud resident of Harrisonburg, VA. Prior to that, I was at the University of Dubuque for six years as an Assistant Professor and the Poet-in-Residence, before that, upstate NY as a

Visiting Professor at Hobart and William Smith Colleges, and before that, in Doha, Qatar (really, wherever the job is!), and the list goes on. I originally came to the US from Trinidad to go to college, and so that was the original adventure, and the others followed from there!

Jeffrey: You originally set out to study medicine but happily for us you decided to switch to poetry; I too, started out as a science major, but then switched to English. Do you recall what it was that compelled you to switch?

Alleyne: Yes, I initially wanted to major in Radiologic Science and Nuclear Medical Technology. I had been a science track student in Trinidad, and have my O-levels in things like Bio, Chem, Informational Technology, and Advanced Math (to name a few). I didn't really want to be a doctor, though (to my parents' chagrin) so I thought RS-NMT sounded more interesting . . . and less bloody. But also, I have a long history with and love of literature. I was an avid reader, I wrote calypsoes for my sister growing up, at O-levels we also had to do English Language and Literature, and I chose to do Literature for A-levels (and I got the highest scores on the island) so I've always held language dear and engaged it in a number of ways. My understanding of university, though, was that it would be a place I would find a career, and RS-NMT was a career; Literature was not. Added to that, my parents had cleaned out their bank accounts, sold their valuables and taken on vast amounts of debt just to get me to New York. Part of the mandate I had given myself was that I would succeed in a way that would help me repay them, and make the same opportunities possible for my siblings. In that way, it was actually an anguish-ridden decision to change my major. It seemed selfish, and irresponsible. I resisted the notion for a long time, thinking I would have my flirtation with English on the side but commit to the sensible choice for a major.

What changed? It was a series of things. It was taking Brother Edward's Honors English class as a freshman, loving it, and then taking every class I could with him after that; it was doing homework with my friend, and realizing the joy she experienced in writing Anatomy reports was more like what I felt when I was writing about Jeanette Winterson's "Gut Symmetries"; it was Brother Edward asking me about my choice in major, and saying to me "Lauren, you were meant to be educated, not trained," and the work my mind had to do to figure out what the distinction meant, and how it would affect my life once I did. Finally, it was going to the orientation meeting for NMT majors at the Kings County hospital, where I took one look at what my days would look like—8 to 5 classes in things I knew I didn't want my life to be composed of, no matter how good I was at doing them. I fled. I went back to the main campus, changed my major, and fretted about what I would tell my mom (who was more resigned than surprised). But I felt so free, and just knew I would never look back. And I haven't.

Jeffrey: I want to talk about your book, *Difficult Fruit*. Indeed, this book takes on some very difficult themes. Obviously, the title takes me back to Billie Holiday's song, "Strange Fruit." There is such a brutal and musical truth in that song, and many of the poems in the first section confront the reality of violence on black bodies. Should readers have this truth in their mind when they read your book?

Alleyne: The truth is I was not thinking at all of Billie Holiday's song. The book had had many titles, but this one I pulled from the long poem, "Eighteen," which I regard as the heart of the collection. Of course, though, once people pointed out that connection, I was not at all sad about those echoes being present for some people. This is a book about the body—the black body, the female body, the body in relationship to the world, and Holiday's song was very much about the black body in relation to the landscapes it inhabited in her time. The resonance is there, and I think it adds another layer to the book that although I didn't intend, I am certainly grateful it is present!

These difficult themes are certainly present throughout the book. To give *LAR* readers a glimpse into that world, here is a small sample from the poem "Ask No Questions":

> Love, the door inside me is locked
> and the bones are begging to be let
> loose with their drums and handbells,
> with their tales of sea at sunrise.
> I confess to the carrying of secrets.
> I confess to bearing songs
> not meant for your tongue.

Jeffrey: In your notes to the poem, "Eighteen," you say that Frances Driscoll's rape poems should be required reading. Why? I confess that I have not read these (but I will).

Alleyne: Driscoll's book is called *The Rape Poems* and that is the first thing that attracted me to it. It was sitting on a friend's bookshelf and I was sleeping on her couch, and I had to get up and look again to see if I had read the spine wrong. To see the word so baldly and boldly written shocked me, and then as I opened the book and read the poems, I was just gripped by the way the poems did not shirk away from the experience of rape, how carefully, lyrically, and brutally, the psychological, physical, emotional effects were laid out. How she managed to then open the book into a cultural and social critique through the recounting of her own experience. But mostly, I think that book made a fissure in a compartment I had long sealed shut—my own experience of a rape in my first year of college. I read that book over and over and over, and each time, it was like a healing, and a confirmation, and though in many ways it was not my experience, it was the closest thing to it I had ever read. Adrienne Rich in "When We Dead Awaken" describes herself "peculiarly susceptible to language" and argues that the lack of strong, substantial female image in literature was particularly harmful to her for this reason.

In many ways, Rich's description felt like a diagnosis for me, but with regards to Driscoll's work, it had the opposite effect. As someone also "peculiarly susceptible to language," Driscoll's poems were able to enter into and connect with a space in my psyche that nothing else had, and they really—no exaggeration here—changed my life. But that's personal. Everyone should read this book, I believe, because there isn't enough (though there is more than there used to be) open discussion about the lived experiences of women who have endured rape. And one way that we can combat the rape culture we live in is to get these stories in their painful diversity and devastating commonality out there in as many ways as possible. Look at the ways in which the letter of the woman who was raped by Brock Turner stirred up consciousness, empathy, and outrage. Testimony is a powerful tool both in recovery and in creating momentum for the possibility of change, and "The Rape Poems" offers it in an important way.

Alleyne's point that testimony is a powerful tool is evident in the poem, "Eighteen"—a litany of light and bodies and battle:

Here is the night snarled with starts, here is the smile full of teeth. Here is the bloom of desire, its scent swift entering everything. Here are the arms, the legs, the heady nectar of lips; here is the nipple erupting against the thicketed chest. Here is the earlobe and thigh, the sharp seduction of nails. Here is naked. Here, light by an exploring moon. Here is heat making a new planet of your heart, riding your blood like victory. Here is the old road you have longed and longed to travel. It hisses your name. Its breath is smoke and salt; it stings your throat like a scream. Here is the trembling gate, and yet you want to turn back, no, run back, to before, which is still now, or could be, if you turn in time and you do, but here are the knots fists makes of fingers, the silence one tongue can shackle to another, the wilful iron of belly and bone. Here is *no*, and *no*, and no answer. Here, shove and bite splinter like so much kindling. Here is laughter sparking mad—jackal, wildebeest, wolf. Here is fire and fire and fire. Skins of flame. Walls of flame. There is no turning here; here you learn how to burn.

Jeffrey: Many of your poems acknowledge the powerful female voices that came before—Lucille Clifton, Jamaica Kincaid, Anne Sexton—how have these women influenced your writing?

Alleyne: In many ways it's back to the "susceptibility" diagnosis. I love a range of poetry, but it was really the poems of women writers that resonated with me on the deepest levels. When I was writing "Eighteen" in particular, but really when I am writing in general, I surround myself with a badass pantheon of poetry patron saints: the women who remind me to be brave and true and strong in my writing. I think it is easy to slip into a "safe" space in writing, but reading women like them—Jan Beatty, Kim Addonizio, Sharon Olds, Toi Derricotte, more recently, Aracelis Girmay and Claudia Rankine—reminds me that risk is not only more rewarding in terms of the poem's craft, but that it is also necessary for the poem to do real work in the world. Rich also says in "When We Dead Awaken," "Our struggles can have meaning only if they can help to change the lives of women whose gifts—and whose very being—continue to be thwarted." I remember how Driscoll cut me open, and helped me heal; I want to do that for my readers (and myself) as much as I can, and I turn to these writers for inspiration and courage.

Healing does seem to be part of the writing process.

Some of the bravest poems in this book are a sort of coming of age series that comes across in poems such as "Seven," "Fourteen," and "Thirty."

From "Seven":

> In this picture, your dress is burning
> white, your veil engulfs your head
> like lacy flames. Your snoopy watch
> flares red on your wrist, you clutch
> your white handbag like a wish.

From "Fourteen":

> How the bud yearns to flower
> believing the bloom is all
> Beauty, perfuming, the bliss
> of pluck. How she snows nothing
> of uprooting

From "Thirty":

> This morning, you start from a dream
> seasoned with bourbon. Last night roils in your stomach,
> funks your breath, aches. A message lights your phone, asking, *Did you get*   *home safe?*

These poems, though not presented in chronological order, follow the journey of a young woman experiencing life at various stages. The one constant though is the scrutiny of the black female body.

Jeffrey: The poems, "John White Defends" and "The Hoodie Stands Witness" both become poems of witness to the injustices of a legal system seemingly stacked against young black men. I wanted to get your thoughts on some of the recent efforts by Black Lives Matter and Mothers of the Movement.

Alleyne: I think the BLM movement has had many successes and is doing amazing ongoing work. What strikes me, though, is that it is really the perfect example of how language can and does move us. What these women were able to do is encapsulate in three words, the whole problem of racial history and racial realities for people of color—black people in particular—in America, the whole weight and depth of it. When Black America heard the phrase "Black Lives Matter," it resonated. It called up something deep and provided a handle on the invisibility, the hopelessness, the struggle that can so often feel so overwhelming and limiting and endless. At the same time, the phrase is a refusal of all of those conditions. It is declarative, it is resilient, and it is an insistence: it demands visibility and justice. It's brilliant.

"The Hoodie Stands Witness" reimagines the hoodie as a last comfort and voice for Treyvon Martin:

> He clung to me then, wholly
> unmanned, a baby clutching
> his blankey. He pulled me close
> and I stroked his head, caressed
> the napps he had brushed into waves
> that morning. I felt him brace
> his bones beneath me, his heart
> a thousand beating drums.
> The bullet ripped through us
> like a bolt of metal lightning.
> His blood, losing its purpose,
> ran into me and I wished
> we were truly a single body,
> that I could have held
> its rush and flow like a second
> sweaty skin. I can tell you
> how his spirit slipped out—
> like steam from cooling water—
> slowly, fading by degrees
> until he stilled.

Jeffrey: The second section of your book is filled with music—how important is the role of music in your writing?

Alleyne: So confession: I'm not a musician. I took ten years of piano and play some guitar, but really, no one needs to hear me, but me! What happened in the second section, is the result of a workshop with Tracy K. Smith, in which she challenged us to do something we'd never done in a poem before. I had never written a sincere love poem, and that became my challenge. I was also in the throes of a turbulent relationship at the time, so writing the poems also turned out to be a good way to sort my heart/head out. But I needed a vehicle—something to help me grasp the abstraction of "love" (shudder), and honestly, I don't remember how I landed on music, but the idea of a relationship as a sonic movement really gave me the vehicle to write the poems. Generally, though, when I think of music in poetry, it really is about how sound propels meaning, how words swing into each other and become dynamic in their own right. I think of Richard Hugo saying the poet makes a decision whether "Truth conforms to music, or music conforms to truth." If I had to choose, I'd say I am in the former camp, but I like to think I try to make each poem a truthful music.

These poems use major chords and minor chords to help make sense of relationships, while "Love in B Major" begins as a series of connections and openings:

> Your hand, sturdy keys
>
> open in me a flock of doors:
>
> I am endless entering.

"Love in B Minor" concludes with blunt force and spaces:

> Do not sing to me. I want to push you out of my heart,
>
> and watch your long fall through its chambers
>
> and valves until you are momentary—a blip,
>
> An irregular beat. Your siren, *please*.
>
> Your face an arrangement of pain. Your face.

Jeffrey: The book ends with a poem giving advice to the fifteen year old self—what advice do you have for fifteen year old girls?

Alleyne: Ah, fifteen. It's an interesting age. Or at least, it was for me. I think what I was struggling with in that moment that I only recognized much later, was the idea of what lay ahead for me. I go back often to Lucille Clifton's "won't you celebrate with me," which is the anthem of my heart. In it, she writes "i had no model / born in babylon / both nonwhite and woman / who did i see to be / except myself." And that's it right there. I loved the people around me, but I couldn't see myself in the life that seemed predestined—finish school; work as a teacher or in a bank or as a civil servant; get married. I didn't even know anyone in my family who'd been to university. But not wanting something isn't the same as knowing what you want, so the future literally felt like I couldn't exist in it, which at the time, I thought meant I would no longer exist. So yes, I literally thought I was going to die before I finished high school. When I kept on being alive, I decided I had nothing to lose, and even though I didn't know what *my* way forward would look like, I moved forward anyway. So my advice for fifteen-year-olds, or young women in general, is to not be afraid to step into the unknown, to embrace what seems impossible, to move into your own path. The barriers and limits are everywhere, but they are not more powerful than your desire, talent, imagination, and determination.

"Fifteen,"

I am writing from 29 to tell you
we live. I remember our dreams,
the long white halls with no end,
and how when we tried to imagine
life after high school, it was blank
and solid as a grave . . .
. . . In two years, we will
step on our first plane, and fall
in love with flight. We will move
like wind across the world: we
conjugate French class verbs in Paris
and Nice; we follow Jesus to Bethlehem,
and Galilee; we have lived places
you do not yet know exist. I see now
that it will all begin with you—
the path away from home marked
with nothing; who could walk it
but the girl who has already made peace
with her own end? 15, looking back,
I understand our quiet death-wait,
the surprise of our persistent daily waking:
We never could have imagined this.

Jeffrey: One of the goals of these conversations is to discuss the challenges of finding time to pursue our craft. How do you juggle the demands of a career and the desire to write? When do you write? What is your process?

Alleyne: Well, this is a perpetual struggle. I'm terribly undisciplined, and don't have set hours, or daily writing routines or anything like that. That said, I generally like long swathes of time to work on a poem. I find it hard to write if I know I will get interrupted, that I won't be able to follow the poem to its end—whether that was five hours or five days. That, of course is difficult to make happen if one wants to have a roof over one's head. As a professor on the schedule of the academic year, I generally guarded my summers vigilantly—I would take workshops, go to residencies, and do as much reading and writing as I could in those months of uninterrupted time so that I would have some drafts to work with. And then I also like to let things sit a while, so I would spend time in the semester editing, and yes, still trying to write, but still having things to work on if that wasn't happening. I'm two days into my administrative role, and so that's one of the things I'm going to have to learn to navigate—having a 9-5, year-round position means that I will have to renegotiate my writing practice, and try something new, which is a little scary, but I've learned to trust that the poems will come when they're ready, and I will make my way to the desk whenever they arrive.

Jeffrey: What is your current project and when can readers expect to read more?

Alleyne: Right now, I'm interested in the idea of home. Three years ago, I became a permanent resident of the US, and this year marks the year I've lived away from Trinidad longer than I ever lived there, so that idea of belonging, place, etc is what's occupying me. I've got drafts of what I've been calling "Tip year poems" in response to that. We'll see what becomes of them. I generally try not to over-determine a project, and just focus on writing the poems.

Right now, though, I'm in recovery from the rigors of the job search—that gruelling cycle of application, interviewing and waiting and teaching while doing so—the move from IA to VA etc. etc. So the writing has been . . . well, slow would be generous. But I'm looking forward, now that I am here in VA and settling in, to getting a writing schedule going, to writing more poems, and seeing where they take me!

Lauren K. Alleyne's book, *Difficult Fruit*, was published in 2014 and is available from Peepal Tree press or through Ms. Alleyne's website, www.laurenkalleyne.com.

AWARDS

SPRING **2016** SELECTIONS:

LAR SHORT FICTION AWARD
LAR FLASH FICTION AWARD
LAR CREATIVE NONFICTION AWARD
LAR POETRY AWARD

AWARDS

HEUN-JEOK

ARAM KIM

—But I'm not done with you, says the wife.

Highest marks go to this masterfully crafted piece. The surreal sorrow met by the wife is in such contrast to the apparent peace achieved by the husband, yet one wonders at the staying power of either. Will not either or both see a reversal of experience in time? The title, which I believe can translate to "trace," "evidence," "vestige," or even "imprint," is pregnant with meaning, and can be seen in the lives of both main characters, the lanterns, and particularly in the bell and what might prove to be the spirit of the bell-maker's daughter. This is a wonderful story. Bravo.

—Tom Janikowski, Final Judge, LAR Short Fiction Award

HE IS NOT A BAD MAN, the husband, she knows. Then who's at fault? Who's to blame?

—Who is he? she asks.

The husband folds origami on the floor—a diamond sharp enough to draw blood, spheres stringed like pearls.

—What's the point? says the husband.

The wife falls to where he's seated. The hem of her skirt catches the spheres stringed like pearls. She buries her face in his clothes and smells him like a mother smelling the hair of her child.

...

The wife knows the man is the head monk at the temple on a cliff at the edge of land. A real, hairless monk, not like the husband washing dishes at the temple kitchen, selling sweetened coffee to worshippers bowlegged after bowing a thousand times. Not long ago, they visited the temple, husband and wife. They watched the great monk dance to music so thin she could hardly watch with a leveled gaze.

—How beautiful it all is, the husband said. —The quiet, the belief.

She nodded, not knowing then that her husband would soon leave her to be a wife to a man serving a lifetime of sacrifices.

From the bottom of the stone steps, the wife catches glimpses of the husband. In linen, his hair pulled into a loose knot. He carries a rubber basin of dishes, bundles of chopped wood, a live chicken by its feet he playfully tickles. His happiness breaks her in two. His happiness she feels from lying next to him all these years, his body curving into hers forever.

There is nothing for the wife to do. She can circle the gravel parking lot. Throw stones into the sea whose winds don't even reach her. She sits inside her car. Eventually starts it and rides down the mountain. To her right is the expansive water. To her left are cliffs veiled in nets to catch drifting rocks. And over the city ahead is a cast of gray ghosts stretched out like nylon over the fields, the kinky motels, the low-tiled roofs housing naked babies humming into each other's ears.

...

When she arrives in the early morning, the temple is still like a scene painted on an old vase. She kicks the piles of collected leaves. She knocks down the stone mounds. She breaks the peace in negligible ways.

A paper door opens. From a prayer room appears her husband who steps out into his humble space. Inside the large stone kitchen, he wakes the fire to warm the back of his beloved monk.

By the time the morning prayers are sung and drums beaten, the monk emerges in his great garb of charcoal draped sadly over his shoulder. Wrapped around a hand are the prayer beads he fingers, one by one by one. Other men and women scrounge around the dirt courtyard. Most of the time, the wife can't figure out who to pay attention to.

When the temple is hushed, the wife finds her way to the husband's bungalow. She imagines him huddled under a thin blanket suitable for a poor man. She calls out, —My darling, Eun. She looks for a place to lean on but finds nothing but darkness. Her body folds, collecting the tired night.

...

The wife walks up the steps. She follows the low hum of prayer to a structure housing the Buddha. The head monk sits with folded legs under him. His hands clasped below his chin, holding the beads.

When he notices her, he says, —You're pretty enough to be a beauty queen.

She finds a place on a cushion of silk. She watches the monk's profile, the closed eyes, the sloping shoulders. She prays herself. In her mind, she tries to describe in words what it is she wants. But what she wants can't seem to be made into words.

After, the wife requests a tour. He shows her the many prayer rooms, the small library filled with books of worship. He takes her to a corner of the temple. Here is a wooden pavilion framing the large bronze bell.

—How has your winter been? the monk asks. He is light and heavy like the moon.

—The coldest in a thousand freezing years, says the wife.

Winter rains begin to pound on the pavilion roof. Mountain mist hangs low.

—You have a nice place here, says the wife. She touches the bell's striker, a thin log suspended from the ceiling by chains.

—How the bell came to be, says the monk, —is a sad story.

—Tell me, she says.

—The first of these bells didn't sound at first, he says. —The head monk of that monastery had seen in his dream for the bell's artisan to sacrifice his own child. And so he did, throwing his only daughter into the melting bronze. Her name was Emile.

—Was it worth it? asks the wife.

—On a crisp day, the bell can be heard as far as five towns over, says the monk. —But, no. I don't think it was worth it.

...

Her car parked in the gravel lot is filled with trash. The tires are buried in thick snow from days of being still.

She searches for leftovers in the stone kitchen. The rest of her day is spent leaning against the pagoda. She calls over a passing boy.

—How do I look to you? she asks. —What's my voice like? Who do you think I am?

When her husband passes by, she whistles. She says, —Looking good. And when all he does is look away, she asks, —Do you like what I've become? Is this what you wanted?

From his place on the top-most platform, the monk watches flanked by stone guards. His garb is endless, the hairless head receiving the only rays of sun under the winter skies.

...

On the night of a full moon, there is a celebration. Paper lanterns are hung on strings across the yard and candles of every size are lighted. Musicians sit on a mat of straw and hum slow songs. Children worshippers throw coins into the well and then drink from it, using the shell of a split gourd.

The wife watches the games being played in circles. When a ball made out of chicken feathers rolls to her, she kicks it back into the circle. She eats the rice cakes spread on a low lacquered table and saves a piece in her pocket. There is a chill in the air no one else seems to notice.

After the festivities, she searches for her husband, the monk. She finds the two in the large open bathhouse. The monk is sitting inside a tub heating over a low fire. And the husband, with a towel, wets the monk's head and back. When the monk emerges from the water, the husband is there to receive him in a large piece of cloth. He is there to dress him back in his great garb of charcoal.

…

—Do you remember me? she asks. —Your wife, Geum?

—Come back to me, she says. —You don't belong here.

There is a light drizzle. The wife sits outside her husband's prayer room. She speaks to him through the closed door.

—I don't know who to be with you here, she says.

—Do you hear me calling at night? she asks.

—Suppose I give everything up. Suppose I tape my mouth shut, she says.

—Was I dumb to believe in everything? she asks.

In the darkness, the rain can't be seen. Only the pit-pat of its landing makes the night less threatening.

—I don't know why I'm doing this, she says. —I'm so embarrassed.

—When I die, will you go with me? she asks. —Will you at least pray for me?

She waits for answers. Long after the night passes and the rain stops. Long after she takes shelter inside the dome of the bronze bell and her cries become one with those of Emile.

After Henry

Barbara Fried

Mine eyes are spent with weeping. —Lamentations 2:11

There is a basic question for all fiction: "What made you want to create this piece?" The judges found the winning entry answered this question with a palpable sense of necessity and urgency. Of course, as in all the best Flash Fiction, every word was essential.

—Ron Koertge, Final Judge, LAR Flash Fiction Award

WHEN HENRY DIED, I STOPPED GOING to the movies. I couldn't see the point. If someone dies, that someone is Henry. If no one dies, then what is it to me? Also, I stopped answering the phone or opening e-mails marked urgent. If they have to find you, they'll find you.

I don't go to museums after noon any more. I want to be long gone when the loudspeaker erupts—a bomb exploding in a safe house—reminding us all that the end is near. I hate that voice. It is the gate clanging shut, the repo man at the door, the last train out before Paris falls.

Before Henry, I loved to walk the city late at night, a proud burgher surveying her demesne, river to river, up and down deserted avenues, past knots of drunken teenagers, street schizophrenics shouting at god, and, complacent fool that I was, I'd think to myself, even here there is life, and hope, or some such sentimental rot.

Now, all I see around me is death: the museum shut up like a grandee's tomb, its entrance bathed in ghastly footlights; the park thrumming with murderous thoughts; restaurants padlocked and dark, save the green glow of the Emergency Exit sign, with its droll promise of salvation. Don't tell me everyone will be back in the morning. Sometimes they won't.

When I detect the telltale signs of a store in trouble, I stop going. I don't want to be there when the *Everything Must Go!!* sign is taped across the front window, its hysterical imperative telling us what we already know. I don't want to see the scuffed-up walls stripped bare, clothes tossed in bins, light fixtures ripped from the ceiling like eyeballs harvested from the dead. I don't want to worry about the people who work there, whether they miss each other, whether they found new jobs, whether they feel like someone they love has died. I want to be able to tell myself that maybe I was wrong, maybe it survived after all.

The day Henry died, I ripped the peonies out of my garden, the bloodroots and sweet peas too. Such profligacy, such great expense for a moment's beauty, flowers blown almost as soon as they are burst. My garden now is made of rock and sow thistle, toad rush and milkweed. It is the color of concrete, the feel of barbed wire and the cool stone monastery floor. It lives on whatever it finds—air, the sound of sirens, yesterday's news. It will still be here in a hundred years, long after we have ceased to haunt anyone's dreams.

And when I see a ten-year-old boy crossing the street, I turn away. If at that moment a driver should lean over to change the radio station, or glance up at the darkening sky, at least I will not be there to witness to it. At least it will not have happened to me.

WINNER OF THE

CREATIVE NONFICTION AWARD

RUPTURE

KIMBERLY MEYER

"Rupture" is an essay in which nothing extraordinary happens—children are born, are mothered, grow up, become independent. The author has the privilege of being home with her kids, and caring for them. It is all very good luck, a sort of controlled experiment within which she explores the deep grief that naturally accompanies motherhood—from the initial rupture of childbirth to their departure as adults. The author does not invent crises. She seeks to connect the ordinary holiness of life with the ancient well of human experience we happen upon when we love someone who we know will eventually not need us, will no longer consume our days. She writes about her daughters' movement away from her as they grow from babies to adults, ". . . something beloved departs from us every day." We worry, even in our moments of happiness, of contentment, that it is not permanent. This is true of all things, but love in particular shifts with its object. It need not be tragic to be profound. She writes: "Though I had no religious rite of passage to perform over them, I wanted nevertheless to mark my first act as their mother with a sign of my devotion, a kind of blessing upon them . . ." "Rupture" connects the ordinary to the divine.

—Seema Reza, Final Judge, LAR Creative Nonfiction Award

WHEN I GAVE BIRTH TO EACH of my three daughters, I did so without any anesthetic, a plucky achievement that surprises me still. I know that natural births have become a kind of status symbol in the new economy of motherhood, like breastfeeding and co-sleeping, which I also did, though I didn't call it that. I just called it "falling asleep in bed with the baby." But that was twenty years ago as I was finishing up college, and no one I knew was having babies yet, so none of this had any cachet that I could trade in. And anyway, it's not the memory of my endurance of the pain of my daughters' births—something animal clawing me open, cleaving me in two—that moves me. It's that I somehow knew even then that their entry into this world would be a violent rupture, and I wanted to feel it as the cataclysm that it was. Though I had no religious rite of passage to perform over them, I wanted nevertheless to mark my first act as their mother with a sign of my devotion, a kind of blessing upon them as they entered this veil of tears: *Here's what I'll suffer for you.*

When my daughters were young, I came upon the writings of the religious historian, Mircea Eliade, who distinguished two levels of existence—the sacred realm and the profane world—for "traditional man" who was, by definition, "religious man," which I'm really not. The profane world is that which our bodies inhabit. In the case of my body, that was a world back then of concrete and crepe myrtles and sidewalk chalk, of baby dolls and goldfish crackers and books at naptime and at bedtime, and a station wagon parked in the driveway of our bungalow. Eliade says that into profane space such as this, at particular places, the sacred erupts, and through the rupture, human beings can communicate with the divine.

The ancient Greeks spoke to their unfathomable gods at the temple of the oracle of Delphi through one such break in the veil marked by an *omphalos*—a hollow, beehive-shaped stone, its surface intricately carved. *Omphalos* means "navel." In the Middle Ages, they called Jerusalem the *omphalos*, the navel of the world, and medieval cartographers placed the Holy City at the center of their maps where, they said, God walked the earth as man. We are, in these sacred centers, connected umbilically to the transcendent.

My ruptured, laboring body was the *omphalos* out of which my daughters had been born—which could make me, if I pushed the metaphor to its logical conclusion, a minor deity, a lesser god. But really, it was my daughters who I worshipped and, in their fickle moods of inexplicable displeasure, attempted to appease. And our home became, I see most clearly now that they are leaving and the site of rupture is closing up, a holy place, alive with meaning—"the only *real* and *real-ly* existing space" in Eliade's phrasing.

What Eliade means is that a sacred space points beyond the material world toward a realm of enduring purpose and significance. What I mean is standing at the kitchen counter trying to cook dinner with a baby on my hip and a toddler at my feet, changing diapers, wiping smeared faces clean, holding little girls just after they've woken from their naps and wandered into the living room, flush-cheeked, looking for me. What I mean is collecting minnows from a tire rut near the street filled with rain water and putting them in a glass bowl with rocks, and splashing in the blue plastic wading pool under the fig tree in the back yard, and pulling out the dress-ups on an empty Saturday afternoon in summer, and picking up the Barbie's and putting them and their clothes and mismatched shoes into the plastic bin at night. What I mean is the tedium of laundry and dishes, the tension between my work at the dining room table late at night and the cry of a daughter, but what I also mean is artwork on the fridge—a line-drawing in crayon of all of us, smiling and in descending height: Daddy, Mommy, Ellie, Mary Martha, Sabine, Matilda the cat.

Our house, with all of us in it, had meaning and purpose. It felt both rooted to the earth and to the tangible and concrete, and at the same time tethered to something beyond, the *real*. It was a place of plenitude and fullness, inhabited by some kind of holy spirit, incarnate in the babbling voices and round bellies of my daughters, bellies I kissed and wanted to consume back in to me. My sister-in-law was telling me the other day about the intense emotional connection she felt to her newborn daughter that was, at the same time, physical, especially when she smelled her, and how she'd read an article about mothers' brains having a similar reaction to their babies' scent as they would sniffing cocaine. So maybe the spirit inhabiting our house wasn't linked to the divine. Maybe it was merely chemical. Or maybe it was just the love between us, a love that went out and came in like breath. At any rate, our daughters felt like saviors. I saw how empty my arms had been before I held them. "You are the one / Solid the spaces lean on, envious," says Sylvia Plath in "Nick and the Candlestick," a poem addressed to her son. "You are the baby in the barn."

In the ancient stories, the gods who do not die cannot know love. No one is dear, meaning precious, meaning costly, because no one can be lost. That's why their endless marriages seem so empty. Zeus is forever disguising himself—as a shower of golden rain, as a swan, as a white bull—and running off with some poor mortal girl, while Hera, ever jealous, is always turning the girl into a beast. The only access the gods ever have to human suffering is when their mortal children die. Gazing down on the dusty plains of Troy as the doom of his son, the warrior Sarpedon, draws near, Zeus considers opposing Fate and saving him. But Hera protests that if Zeus plucks out his own child, the other deathless ones will want to save their sons too, and then where would they be? Mostly, though, human beings aren't worth the bother. They are, says Apollo to Poseidon, "like leaves, no sooner flourishing, full of the sun's fire, feeding on earth's gifts, then they waste away and die."

Love can only exist in the presence of death. That's what Odysseus knows as he sits weeping on the shore of Calypso's island, aching to return to his mortal wife, Penelope, and to rocky Ithaka with its goats and grapevines and heavy dews, and to his son, a suckling child when he left years before for the war at Troy, now a boy trying desperately to become a man. The perfection of the immortal Calypso bores him. So does immortality itself, a gift the goddess offers Odysseus, but which he rejects for the wife and son and high-roofed hall of home that will one day pass away.

But death comes in many forms. It's not only the abstract and hopefully distant end that will occur when our bodies die. Watching babies become little children who become teenagers who put on their headphones and close their doors and grow quiet reading their own books and then leave taught me that something beloved departs from us every day. All those years, I had tried to pay attention. I took pictures. I wrote down what my daughters said, as if their utterances were those of the sibyls, ears to the *omphalos* at Delphi, umbilicus to the gods, which I could mine for meaning and direction. But our house now feels drained of the numinous, like hardened coral pulled by the roots from the vast sea that once animated it, if coral had roots and the sea was transcendent.

Sometimes in this lost space of grief that has opened me up, I wonder: those years when my children filled our house with their holy spirits, were they only a brief reprieve from the loneliness that always lurks beneath? Did my daughters' presence rupture the darkness momentarily—the darkness that's encroaching again now? Is that darkness "the only *real* and *real-ly* existing space"?

But other times, I think that this grief must surely be a liminal space—liminal, which comes from the Latin for "threshold." I'm standing in a doorway between here and there, like the doorway my daughters passed through to this world as I blessed them with my pain. I want to figure out how to make this pain of their departure a blessing too. Through the threshold, I can just make out the distant hills. Beyond them, who knows? I'm trying to figure out in which direction to start walking.

ON BEING ASKED WHAT QUESTION I DON'T WANT TO ANSWER

REBECCA BROWN

Why did I select this poem? The speaker in "On Being Asked What Question I Don't Want to Answer" dances with the darker themes of violence and despair with prowess, levity, and a wit that guards against the sentimental. It's an engaging poem all the way through—a poem of urgency and invitation, a poem that rides with the mind's associations. Cherry tomatoes, hotel sheets, god-terror, cicadas—the house of memory is summoned here in strange and non-linear ways. Constructed of fragmented answers to unknown questions—questions that by the title's frame are undesired—the poem puts me off-kilter, and I like that. I'm carried along by the rhythms and repetitions—"I say yes desperately. I say chestnuts"—though the full story remains artfully obscured. As a reader, I feel, in this poem, the self coming alive into its own confusing existence—an awakening to the past as it lives in the present, and an attempt to reckon with the holiness and terror that live beneath the surface of things.

—Brynn Saito, Final Judge, LAR Poetry Award

I say for what. I say don't
you have your own life to deliberate. I say Pravin
and 25. I think of the lilac
bush in the alley behind our house.
I say because she tried when I was drunk
and singing karaoke very badly. I say
cherry tomatoes. I think of the dust kicking
up from the white-washed gravel.
I say perspicacity. I say Jesus fuck.
I say when I lay in bed and was terrorized
by the idea of eternity. I say god. I say fish.
I think of the tree in the yard with the empty shells
of cicadas decamped for the next town

and its Dairy Queen. I say her
hand on my back. I say the first thing I knew
was I would hurt other people. I say *The Bear*.
I think of how I almost strangled myself with a sheet
at the Blueberry Hill Motel.
I say yes desperately. I say chestnuts.
I say chicken bone and Jeff Brubaker. I say the laminated
green tile floor of our bathroom. I think of singing *Cherish* in the car
with the world black around us and the green dashboard
holy as dragonflies. I say milk. I say sloe-eyed.

FICTION

FICTION

Stories about Men

Rhian Sasseen

THIS STORY DOES NOT PASS THE Bechdel test. This story has been told before, and will be told again. It has a narrow scope, a simple focus; it's the distance between two fingers, the length of two skeletons conjoined. A pattern, a rhythm. Hormones. Sighs.

What I'm trying to tell you is this: All a relationship really is, when it boils down to it, is an exchange. You let me into your head, and I'll let you see inside of mine. From there, it's up to you how you react to what you find.

...

When I left my husband, I was suddenly overtaken by the need to sleep with every new man I came across. Well, not every man, only those I found attractive. And while this encompassed the men who were, by definition, "my type"—however nebulous a distinction that is—it mostly included those who exuded a particular quality, an ineffable *something*, that seeped from each pore like a perfume. What would we call this in a woman?—Desperation. That's it.

At first, I resisted. Even in the twenty-first century, a woman with a careless attitude toward sex can find herself thrust within one of two categories: the despondent or the slut. Neither one appealed to me. The latter was just offensive, while the first bored me, being as it was a familiar tale: a troubled yet intelligent woman somehow loses everything (her identity? her standards?) through the self-flagellation of intercourse with strangers and, in doing so, discovers something important about human nature. I'd watched it before in a thousand art-house films, read it in a million pale and smug little essays; no thank you, said I. I was not attempting to achieve some mystical nirvana born from the rhythms of a stranger's body; I rather like who I am, and besides, this idea that sex for women always has to be *about* something was exhausting. I was not attempting to efface myself. I was not attempting to explore an untapped dark side, or exact moral revenge against my ex-husband and/or my parents, or even to stick a finger toward the patriarchy. It was just that, every night I woke up slick and anxious, and felt as though I would die if I didn't fuck someone right then and there. *End scene.*

Months passed. My divorce stalled, then sputtered up again, with new life breathed into the reality of our separation once Justin fell into bed with a stranger all his own. I lived first with my brother and my sister-in-law, then with a friend, and then finally moved into an apartment of my own. At work, I received a promotion. On weekends, I went out with friends or co-workers or my sister-in-law or sometimes even my mother. I constructed patterns, and I stuck to them.

"You should try dating again," my sister-in-law told me one evening when I explained this to her. It was the first warm night of the season, and every restaurant in the city was cluttered with optimists, clad in too-short shirtsleeves and ordering sangria by the pitcher. Donna Summers was playing on the stereo. Everyone was smiling, pretending it was warmer than it was; we were actively mythmaking, all of us, each table filled with people convincing one another that the night was beautiful, the room was beautiful, that everything and everyone was beautiful, full to bursting, and ripe. But it was only April.

"I know a guy," my sister-in-law persisted, "who also just had a breakup."

"Maybe," I told her, sipping my drink. A few chunks of jalapeño floated amidst the wine, and they burned my throat not unpleasantly as I drank. Our server came along and though we quickly changed the conversation, the thought persisted. *What if,* I imagined, and found myself attracted to this idea, this type: this brash single woman entering the world on her own terms. When I went home that evening, I sat in front of my computer and started a dating profile. One hand rested near the front of my jeans. As I looked online, dreaming, it began to move almost unconsciously, drawn, as always happens when I am alone, to the heat of me: that longing.

...

"You two look," Justin's mother told us mere moments before her sister-in-law's third wedding, "like something out of a John Cheever novel."

It was late August, and we were as of yet still unwed. Justin wore a navy linen suit that night, while I was also in something blue, a silk Steven Alan dress I had purchased at a sample sale earlier that month. As the evening progressed, we drank nothing but gin, tempered only by a thimbleful of tonic for taste; pearls glinted from my ears. Throughout the reception, every member of his family came up to us and asked when we'd be next.

The following year, as it would turn out. That night—another August—there was another silk dress, albeit in white; another suit for Justin, albeit this time in black. There was gin, again, in copious amounts. Pearls glinted from my ears.

Husband, wife. The words carried with them an air of finality. Halfway through the dancing, I excused myself to sit down for a moment and massage my heeled feet. We had strung up small white lights all around the venue, and under their soft glow the world looked romantic. Justin's brother sat down next to me and offered another glass of champagne, which I accepted. "Cheers," he said, and we clanged. "Welcome to the family."

I sipped the champagne and watched my own parents dancing, my own brother laughing with the girlfriend who would years later become his wife. My own family, no longer. The story of heterosexuality is the story of familiarity; I didn't know it at the time, but I was being transmogrified that evening into something else entirely, shaped like clay into Galatea.

I took another sip and excused myself with a smile.

"There you are," Justin said, enveloping me into a hug and spinning me around. His groomsmen, old college friends, cheered; my bridesmaids, my own old friends, had formed the type of dance circle I remembered from our student days, backs turned toward everyone else as they waved their arms wildly in their own private enjoyment. Under the soft lights, there was the pink blush of their dresses, the silver of their shoes. Their laughter.

"This is my wife," Justin said proudly to a cousin, relishing the phrase. I smiled and waved; I was happy. The whole night was beautiful: the flowers, the lights, the ceremony. The love was beautiful. But still, a small part of me remembered.

That other reception, a year before—as the liquor burned through me, and as Justin's hand burned at the low of my back, the plot flickered in and out. How to explain, I wondered—I wasn't even fully aware of it myself—how to explain that the writer we were imitating, however unconsciously, wasn't Cheever—wasn't Updike—definitely wasn't Roth—her name, in fact, was Victoria Lucas?

The wedding continued. The marriage continued. Years passed. "A circle and a line," I later read in a book about desire, "defined a debate in sexology, a debate about the natural course and velocity of female desire, a dispute entangled with a question: how well do marriage and monogamy work for women's libidos?"

Wouldn't he like to know, I thought, and surprised myself by tearing out the page. Later, when I returned this book to the library, it remained intact save for that single page, a hidden stopgap: the monstrous feminine, indeed.

...

"So you've been here before?" the man across the table asked. He gestured vaguely around the main room of the cocktail bar where we were seated, and I took another sip of my drink before answering. "Yes," I told him, and neglected to say that it had been with another man.

I was trying to be charming. I was trying to be nice. I had no real reason to be here, no real reason outside of the fact that I was bored and I wanted to fuck. Is that cynical to admit? I wondered. Months of listening to my sister-in-law's advice, of putting myself out there and attempting to be some form of "free" had led to this; if only we could be honest with one another, I wished, not for the first time. But enough men had implied to me that, though I said I didn't want anything serious, really, *I did*, as though they knew me better than I knew myself.

And by now I knew the prattle, I knew the pattern. We'd start with introductions and then head into jokes, veer toward our alma maters and stop briefly at our hobbies; along the way, he'd probably pay the bill and I'd probably head back to his apartment. The time had come, now, to listen to him speak about his life without letting it slip that I had looked him up online earlier that evening, and now already knew too much.

"And you do something with computer software, right?" I asked.

"Yeah," he said, and launched into a tedious explanation.

I looked around the room. It was a Friday night, and the bar was already crowded with couples. Some looked at ease with one another, already established, and familiar with one another's tics and vices; most did not. The room was cavernous and dark. At the table beside us, a woman laughed awkwardly; at another, one man checked his phone surreptitiously as the man opposite him told a story. Snatches of conversation puffed around the room before they were swept away by the jostling bodies of the wait staff or patrons. "Some people," I had a chance to hear a girlish voice sigh, "just fit with their married names—"

A hostess sailed past, cutting her off. I wondered what she'd think of mine.

After this night, I'd meet with friends over drinks, and they'd beg me for stories. "I'm so glad I'm not single," the coupled ones would laugh, before asking me for the most explicit of details: size, shape, positions . . . I'd oblige, turning ugly, and spin a tale of caricatures: the bumbling man, the disappointed woman. We'd laugh again. "More!" they'd urge, and so I'd head out once more into the night.

Our second round arrived. "You look thoughtful," this man teased, leaning closer.

I smiled. "Oh, I'm just enjoying myself."

...

"Perception shifts," read the gallery note located near the art show's entrance, "depend on where we place our bodies inside the artist's professional structure." The man beside me snorted. "Density," the note continued (I flushed red with irritation at his laugh), "gives way to diffusion. Forms reflect and multiply."

"Wow," the man beside me said while gazing over at the artwork, composed of thousands of multicolored strings strung taut from floor to ceiling. "They can really call anything art these days, can't they?"

We moved through the strings like fish through a whale's baleen teeth. Beside us, the other black-clad museumgoers filtered through, and I wondered why I had slept with him the night before, why I had said yes to his suggestion to go to the museum. The strings around us seemed almost to vibrate, to shimmer. (*No, no, no*, he had said, leaning back in an awkward attempt to tease, or dominate.) It looked almost as though they moved. (He sat back on his heels, interrupting the flow of our bodies, and shook a finger at me like a chiding schoolteacher.)

"Wouldn't it be funny," he said, pointing toward the center of the gallery, "if someone just took their bed and set it there and said, hey, it's art?"

(*So take me, then*, I had finally cried out, if that was really what he wanted. The whole charade frustrated me. He blinked, as though confused that I had, eventually, acquiesced to join his fantasy.)

"Someone already did. In the '90s."

"Of course there's already been one, I should have known."

"It was brilliant."

He looked at me askance. "Do you really think that?" In the next room, we drifted toward opposite sides, and by the time we had reached the permanent collection, I sat down in front of a Kandinsky and lost him entirely.

It was better here. Though the modernism wing was always busy, most of the crowds seemed more concerned with the cubists than the Russians. I watched my fellow patrons stream in and out for what felt like hours, or minutes; time moves differently inside of a museum.

A little girl and her mother stopped beside me, holding hands, and considered the painting for a while. "The colors," I heard the girl say to her mother, who agreed.

"What's the painting about?" she asked. Her voice was very small.

Her mother shrugged and squeezed her hand. "It doesn't have to be *about* anything," she said. "It's just a painting. It's whatever you want it to be."

They stood there for a few minutes more before moving on. I sat there for a while longer, and dwelled on each color, each brushstroke, each word that had led me to this point in time.

...

Call me Isabel, call me Anna. Call me Emma Bovary. In the last year of my marriage, I often found myself as heartsick as she.

It's not as though we didn't try. We were aware of the problems that had plagued our parents' marriages, our grandparents', the whole damn institution; we understood that certain expectations were associated with marriage and we were confident that we could dispel them. Justin did the laundry, while I always drove. But these were cosmetic solutions. The real problem ran much deeper.

It was the way that at parties, I was somehow treated as an aside. During holidays, when Justin's father once told me that, in an earlier and more fortunate time, my husband would have been able to take care of me. One weekend at a beach house with a friend of Justin's and his girlfriend, during which they'd retreat in the middle of the day to a bedroom and the halls would soon be filled with the cliché of her budget Ishtar wails, of his conspicuous silence. Though we insisted that we were aware of the plot, that we knew the story, it became clear that so did everyone else, and while we were attempting to resist it, they had bought into it all along. Soon, I found myself doing the same; without realizing it, I picked up after him, I nagged, I planned for his dreams and future. One day I woke up and realized that I didn't understand the man lying in bed beside me, I didn't know who he was beyond my husband. And if he was only my husband, then I was only his wife.

I shouldn't have had the affair. I shouldn't have strayed—but, then again, what is literature beyond the stories of cheating wives? When that man standing beside me at the birthday party shrugged and confided, "I don't really understand what women see in men," I had to show him.

"How was the party?" Justin called out sleepily when I returned later that night.

My hands shook as I removed my pearl studs. "Oh, great, you know Casey." In the dark all men look the same. "She's such a social butterfly, I don't know how she does it." A story is an action; a book, a life, is simply a series of actions.

"Yeah, you smell like cigarettes," he teased as I climbed into bed. He pulled me toward him, his bare nostrils tracing my naked shoulder. His arms wrapped around me. "And other people's cologne."

I stiffened. "The bar was really packed. We were like sardines in there."

"I figured." He kissed my ear lobe. I moved away.

In the morning, I couldn't get out of bed. "My poor hungover wife," he laughed, petting my brow. "I'll grab some water." I spent the day lying there, sick and feeble. I closed my eyes and burrowed deeper beneath our pillows, the red of my eyelids the red of his hair, the red of my heart and the red of my despair.

My story is: destroy the plot.

BLOODY STEAK

MEHDI M. KASHANI

IN THE JOB INTERVIEW, WHEN ASKED why waitressing, I'd responded with what Melissa had advised me to say: *I like working with a variety of people.* Cliché as it was—and putting aside the fact I needed the money—it was indeed a truthful answer.

Granted, Bellingham Airport, built for its namesake city of about eighty thousand, is no Heathrow. You won't find as many interesting people. Actually far from it. But in the past month or so, since I started working at Scotty Brown, the only decent restaurant after the security checkpoint, days rarely slipped into nights without meeting a couple of remarkable customers. If you approach everything with open eyes and a curious mind keen for surprises, you'd be surprised what you find.

Such was my attitude when I walked that lone man to a corner table. He had brown skin with raven-black hair, though some parts of his carefully trimmed beard had turned white. Navigating through the tables was usually when I asked where my customers were traveling.

"Back home. LA!" he said while removing his laptop bag from around his neck and placing it on the seat next to him.

"Oh! I got my bachelor's from USC," I said, well aware of how common experiences can ignite conversations.

"Then you know how we spoiled Californians are allergic to rain."

I apologized for the weather outside, as if I had caused it.

"After checking my luggage at the counter and the security search, how pleasant it is to sit in a cozy restaurant, chatting with such a lovely lady!"

I couldn't place his accent but he appeared to be Arab. There was a strange cadence in his tone, an exaggerated emphasis on his T's.

I smiled, gazing down. Many people had flattered me about my appearance, yet there was a sort of modesty hidden in the man's words that distinguished them from the admiration of young men I would meet at bars and clubs.

I put the menu on the table. The man took a precursory glance at the list and, as if he had already made up his mind, put his finger on the words Top Sirloin.

"This morning I managed to close an important deal in Vancouver. What do you say if I treat myself to a steak?"

"Excellent choice! How do you like it cooked?"

He wanted it medium-rare, next to a glass of Pinot Noir. On my way to the kitchen, I noticed a family of four being seated at a table nearby. In the kitchen, the cooks were idle. I passed them the man's order, poured the wine and was about to find a steak knife when I was interrupted.

"Seattle, New York, London, Barcelona, Cairo, back to Seattle! Sixteen hundred, ninety-nine before tax. How can you beat that?"

It was Melissa, enunciating cities and numbers like a travel agent.

"I probably can't." I placed the wine glass on a tray. "I can't afford the trip. Yet."

"But it's for three months from now. You have time to save your tips. We really should buy the tickets though. What a price!"

Melissa always insisted on buying tickets as soon as possible. Every other day, she would come to me with a new route and a tantalizing deal. Her recent breakup with her boyfriend from our USC days had only heightened her penchant for travel, but changing its goal from discovery to recovery. This time the price was as alluring as the itinerary was tempting.

"Let me think about it."

"Think faster!" she yelled as I left the kitchen with the tray and four menus for the family.

Up until that point, I had only travelled along the West Coast, always staying in the same time zone. New York! London! Barcelona! Cairo! These names had always been no more than abstract concepts and now they were gaining new significance. An old dream was about to be realized.

I delivered the menus, then arranged the lone man's cutlery and napkin before him. Then I served him his drink.

"The name of my eldest daughter is Emily, too." The man's eyes sparkled at my nametag.

I smiled, struggling to find something nice to say. "How old is she?"

"She's in her rebellious teenage years, you know, can't hold a meaningful conversation with her parents to save her life."

"We've all been through that phase, haven't we?"

"Except that I was punished with a belt when I was her age." He chuckled. "You live in this town, Emily?"

"Yes! Bellingham is my hometown. Where are you from?"

"Originally from Iran, but it's been eighteen years since I have been living in the States, close to where you studied."

"You speak Arabic then."

The man frowned.

"The language of Iran is Persian. Has always been," he paused, calming down, "Not that I have a problem with Arabs, it's that it is not our language. We have such a rich Persian heritage, you know, that it hurts our pride when someone ignores it."

He started talking about Persian culture and mentioned poets I'd never ever heard of. I'd always spent so much time learning about different cultures that not knowing that Iran's language was Persian embarrassed me. The man wrapped up his soliloquy, stressing that I should take a trip to Iran.

"I'd really like to. As a matter of fact my friend and I are saving to visit Europe and North Africa."

"You should do it. And you should extend it to more places. You'll learn by traveling, not only by a university degree."

"I wish I didn't have to pay back my loans. . . ."

"There's a Persian proverb that literally goes, *money is the pus coming off the hand*, which roughly means," he paused, narrowing his eyes.

"Money comes and goes," I suggested.

"Cheers to that!" he lifted his wine glass.

There was a certain kind of mannerism in his behavior. He seemed to be as proud of his nationality as of his assimilation to this country.

The man in the next table, the family of four, waved at me, probably ready to order. My conversation time was almost up.

"How I wish Emily, my Emily, had your passion," the Persian man said wistfully. "I keep telling her, she should taste the world before attending college. She isn't even curious about Iran, where her roots are."

"I wasn't curious at her age either. I'm sure she will be in due time, having such an encouraging father." Presuming I was compassionate enough, I continued, "Now, if you'll excuse me . . ."

He didn't seem to hear me though. He started talking about traveling: how it opens up new horizons, how it breaks stereotypes, how it stirs dialogues and dispels misunderstandings, and other words of wisdom that I'd heard many times before. Yet, I listened out of courtesy—and also to make up for my ignorance.

As soon as he took a deep breath, I excused myself. I found the neighboring table was on the same plane as the Persian man. They had two young daughters, both hungry and throwing tantrums.

In the kitchen, the steak was ready. The cook placed it in the middle of a plate, garnished with mashed potatoes and chopped carrots. In the dining room, the man's ravenous eyes followed the plate as I gently placed it in front of him. He thrust his fork into the meat.

"Perfecto!"

"Bon appétit! Anything else you might need?"

"A sharp knife and I promise I won't bother you again."

I looked down at the table. I thought that I'd already brought him his knife. The cardinal rule of airport restaurant service was to keep track of the knives. Within the transit area, it was forbidden to provide knives for most meals. Steak was the exception. All knives were numbered to ensure easier tracking. I returned to the kitchen to find another steak knife, scanning the floor, hoping to spot the first one. But I found nothing.

To comply with the rules, I had to immediately advise Melissa, who in turn had to inform airport security. We'd been told to take no chances. After my report, the man would probably be searched again. This time, it would be more aggressive. There was a good chance that he would miss his flight.

The man was carefully chopping steak into square portions, unmindful of his being watched. What were the odds this serene man would conceal a knife in his pocket and then use it to threaten the lives of his fellow travelers in less than an hour? Had his chatter been designed to deceive me? To gain my trust? Did he really have a daughter named Emily, if any?

I supposed it was all possible, and yet I couldn't believe he was an assassin. If that friendly conversation hadn't been sparked between us, would I be in this situation? Had I paid closer attention to my job, I'd have known for certain whether I'd given the man a knife. My mistake could easily jeopardize my career and my trip—not only mine, Melissa's too.

At last the family's order was ready. I balanced their plates on my inner arms and walked carefully toward them. The girls were impatiently waiting for their food. They were a beautiful family, like the ones hired for TV commercials. And they were his fellow passengers. I placed the steaming food before them. When I passed the man's table, he asked for his bill. His steak was gone, only stains of red blood remained.

I ran to the kitchen and examined the cutlery drawer. Out of fifteen steak knives, eleven were in place. I examined the other restaurant patrons. Other than the Persian man and the family I was serving, two old women sat at the bar drinking wine. I opened the dishwasher and bent over the silverware bin to hunt for knives. My coworkers stared at me. In the pile of cutlery, I found two more knives. Still one knife was missing.

I left the kitchen. The mother of the two girls was stirring her younger daughter's food. Meanwhile, her husband was teasing the older one as she tied her long blond hair in a ponytail. The Persian man was talking on his cell. I felt Melissa's eyes on me as I wondered who the man was talking to.

"He wants his bill," I said.

"And?"

"One of the steak knives is missing."

Melissa's eyes grew wide. She was more experienced. She knew what a disaster this could lead to.

"Why didn't you mention it earlier? Prepare his bill while I call security. But make sure he doesn't get suspicious. Don't forget to smile."

She didn't wait for me to respond.

"What if I was wrong?" I yelled as she went to her office.

She dragged me to a corner, where no one could see us but we could still watch the man.

"I don't want to sound racist or xenophobic or anything. But look, he's obviously an Arab," she pointed at him. "Doesn't it all fit too conveniently?"

"He's Persian, not Arab."

"Even worse!" she said indignantly and then continued after a pause. "If you are wrong, you'd owe a few people an apology for taking their time. And if you are not wrong, you'd save the lives of hundreds."

"Maybe someone in the kitchen needed a knife. . . ."

Melissa turned to me. She looked resolute.

"Try to understand, Emily! There's not much time. The airline is already boarding his flight."

I inhaled deeply and brought the man his check and a small candy in a tiny wooden tray. Feigning a smile, I claimed his dirty knife.

The man thanked me. "You look hurried."

"Sorry!" I mumbled, afraid the tremble in my voice would betray me.

"I wanted to tell you that Emily in Persian means *intelligent*. It was very tough for us to find a name that resonates so well in both our cultures."

"Oh! Interesting!"

I had to leave before the police arrived.

Four men from Homeland Security entered the restaurant. It seemed the one in the lead held the highest rank. Since I didn't have the guts to stare at the spectacle, I leaned against the kitchen wall and listened to the exchange. One of the cops asked the man to go with them to be searched.

"I just came from there," he replied.

I figured he'd be worked up but his tone was calm, though a bit surprised.

"I understand! There are some complications that require you to go through the process again."

"Where in the world are passengers taken from a restaurant to be searched again?"

"I am sorry, sir! We have reports that you might be carrying a knife."

My blood ran cold. I felt betrayed by the cops. I'd been hoping that with some absurd miracle the topic of the knife would never be brought up and the man would cooperate without asking questions. What was he thinking now? What was he thinking about *me*? It was as if I'd broken the rules of friendship. I sat down and hugged my knees.

"Gentlemen, I am a citizen of this country. I work for an American company. The Constitution has given me the right to defend myself. What you are doing is insulted . . . I mean insulting . . . and absolutely unjustifiable. If the restaurant has made a mistake and a knife is missing why should *I* be held responsible?"

"According to the amendments of the same Constitution, I am entitled to use my own discretion to save the lives of passengers traveling through American air space. Please cooperate or I'll have to use force."

"Your discretion comes about because I have a Middle Eastern look to me, doesn't it?"

For a few seconds there was silence. He was too proud to voluntarily cooperate. I knew him enough to vouch for that.

"For the last time, I am asking you to come with us."

I stuck my head out of the kitchen to witness the man's reaction. The man was seated, motionless, observing the cops. To my surprise, the family of four was still there too. Each parent had one girl on their lap. With the first cop's signal, two others grabbed the man's arms and lifted him up. The fourth cop had bared his Taser and was monitoring the proceedings. The man didn't resist. Instead, he reluctantly followed the cops. The one in charge claimed the man's belongings—cautiously.

I didn't budge from where I was hiding until Melissa asked me to clean off the man's table. I obeyed. The mother still had her youngest in her arms. Her husband smiled at me.

"You did the right thing," he said, sipping from his beer.

I could no longer draw the line between right and wrong and I certainly didn't want to discuss it.

I went directly to the man's table. The plate was quite clean except for the bloody, red stains. The prongs of the fork also had the red marks. The man had paid in cash: a fifty-dollar bill was in the tray. I wondered if he would have asked for change, or if he'd intended to leave such a generous tip. With what had happened, it would have been only fair if he hadn't left me a penny. Under a deluge of conflicted feelings, I picked up the wooden tray. Under the tray I found a hundred-dollar bill, so new that I had to use my thumb and index fingers to pick it up. Next to Benjamin Franklin's headshot, in handwriting that demonstrated he was not a native English speaker, the man had written, "For Emily, bon voyage" in blue ink.

THINGS DEMONS SAY
AFTER BEING EXORCISED
KELLY MAGEE

That was dry clean only.

Do you have your receipt?

Do you know your policy number?

I'll transfer you.

File not found.

Do you work here?

That's our other location.

Your appointment was for next week.

That's not covered.

We have no record of that transaction.

Do not refresh this page.

Are you sure you want to do that?

Password changed.

Which one are you?

Did you order this?

Your card was declined.

It was your best friend.

It was your sister.

Have another glass.

One more won't hurt.

I didn't plan it.

I got the results.

I'm not judging you.

Is it wrong to say?

I'm not racist but.

That was bad.

I read your texts.

I didn't see you there.

We need to talk.

Unfortunately this piece did not fit.

What was your name again?

Just Ask for Hateman

Laurie Ann Doyle

IT'S LIKE THERE'S THIS INVISIBLE WALL between us. My father's still in park but now he's got this blue recycling bin parked out in front of him. He pulls out a crushed Coors can, a Gatorade bottle, and a dirty wine jug, putting each on the ground carefully. He stares at me across the street—my heart almost bursts through my chest—then away. Of course he doesn't recognize me. It's been forty years since my father and I last saw one another. He's grown thin in that time, his beard white and scraggly. But his shoulders aren't hunched like you usually see in old men. He's wearing this floppy hat and it's covered with buttons: blue, green, black flashing in the morning sun. What looks like a leopard skin thong twists around the hat band. I want to walk across the street but my feet won't go.

"Ma'am?"

The voice is deep and has the authority of a policeman. I've seen cops in the park, too, walking stiff-legged across the wet grass and hassling anyone who gets in their way. When I turn around, that's what I see—a policeman, a tall man in dark blue bearing down on me. Then I realize the deep-set eyes are staring more at one another than me, and his feet are half-shoved in their shoes, the heels bouncing. His legs stop moving for a moment and the eyes focus in.

"You have a beautiful chin," he says.

I've never thought of my chin as anything but bony, too skinny like the rest of me.

He nods. "You've been by. I noticed. More than once."

Back in Ohio, I thought it would be easy. *Just walk up and say, "Hey, Dad. It's me, Toni."* Or Smudge or Pesto or Briar or any one of the names he gave me. Names I never heard out loud but read scrawled across postcards that my mother hid. I brought a few with Dad's ant-like black handwriting. The thing is I've been in Berkeley three days now and can't get closer to my father than ten feet.

The tall man grins. "Why?" Now one of his big shoulders is jumping. "I mean, with ears like that."

What is he talking about? Chin? Ears? His sunburned fingers touch my arm but I don't step away. He's strange, but strange I had been expecting. His smell isn't bad, a musty too-long-without-a-shower smell. His hands are clean. He probably knows my father, the man the rest of the world calls Hate.

He took off when I was seven, moved to California, and developed this philosophy, religion, ideology—nobody knows what to call it. He used to stand in Sproul Plaza yelling *I hate you!* Amazingly, people laughed. After a while, a student reporter at the *Daily Cal* took notice. "Hate is caring," he told her, "as opposed to indifference. Indifference is the problem." Later someone from the *Oakland Tribune* followed him around for a day. "If we can be honest," he said, "straight about the negative feelings we all have for one another, then we can have a real conversation. We can care." A Hate Camp sprung up in the park.

"You tired?" the man says, still staring at me. "Because I am. We all are. What with life." He stops jiggling for a moment and smiles. "Maybe I could help."

I am so tired, but I shake my head.

"So where are you from? Nobody in Berkeley is from Berkeley."

"Ohio," I say. "A little town called Monroe." The truth is I was born in New York City and lived there till I was seven. Monroe's my mother's hometown, the place she moved us to after my father left. I don't feel like I'm from anywhere.

"I was from Milwaukee once. Now I'm from here. Berkeley's a lot better than people give it credit for." He stretches out his hand. "Name's Krash. With a *K*."

I touch his palm. "You don't know someone called Hateman, do you?"

"Sure. Good man, Hate. Helps handle all the crazy shit that flows into the park."

"He's my—"

"Hate," he yells without letting me finish. "Hate! Someone here to see you!"

My father doesn't seem surprised. He walks around a mud puddle and sits on a warped bench. He motions to the empty place next to him with a blank smile.

My hair's short and gray now, not black and pulled into a long braid running down my back. The last time he saw me, I wasn't skinny at all.

He waves at me again.

My heart starts banging in my chest, but now my feet take me across the street. Oak trees line the corner of the park where my father sits. People lie with their heads buried in sleeping bags and someone's scattered cook pots around. When I get closer, a man sits up suddenly, startled. I keep walking. The air smells like incense, heavy and too sweet. Then maybe weed. The grass is slick from last night's rain.

When my father first arrived in California, one newspaper said, he rented a room off Telegraph Avenue. Then he camped out in some bushes on campus, or slept in the corner of a heated garage when it rained. But he was always hanging out in People's Park, so thirteen years ago he moved outdoors permanently. "I'm not homeless," he told the reporter. "I mean if I didn't want a BMW, would you call me BMW-less?"

Alongside the bench are his belongings, plastic bags spilling out of paper bags, torn spiral notebooks, two tuna-fish-can ashtrays. An extra pair of shoes sits nearby, one black, one white. For oppositionality, I know. Hate as opposed to love. A battered *Webster's Dictionary* with HATE CAMP Magic-Markered across the cover holds down the corner of a wrinkled tarp. My father worked at the *New York Times* for ten years: first copy boy, then reporter, then Metro Desk editor. Both newspapers made a big point of that.

I sit down on the bench next to my father. My hand's shaking so bad I have to hide it under my leg. Forty years. He pulls out a pair of scissors tied inside his pocket with a long string, snips off the filter of a Virginia Slim, and inhales. Deeply. He has that smoky *Dad* smell I suddenly remember loving.

He exhales a slow breath. "Before we begin—" I know what he's going to say. Every conversation has to start with *I hate you.* "You don't have to mean it," he tells me, "but it'll be there when you need it. Which you will—because sooner or later we all feel contempt for one another." My father goes on, speaking quickly, softly, as if he's said just these words in just this way to millions of people. And I'm one of the millions.

Until eight months ago, I didn't think much about my father. The ache of missing him had gone or just become part of me. But in June, my mother died. Cleaning out her house, I discovered a Keds box hidden under the bed filled with postcards my father had sent me. For years they'd kept coming, postcards she had never shown me. I found a file folder, too, full of yellow newspaper clippings. I read everything quickly, feeling happy that he'd cared, then guilty, as if my mother were standing right behind me.

Then, angry. Why hadn't she told me?

I looked at the card of my father standing in front of the Campanile, one hand perched on his hip and smiling. *Why not?* I thought. *Why not just take a week and see?* Without my mother living across town now, my life felt empty.

He's still talking. Maybe I should hand him the postcard of palm trees and surf I'd brought. Or say, *Dad, stop. It's me.* But I still can't make myself reach through the silence of decades, the separation I'd always assumed was permanent. In Monroe when people asked, sometimes I told them he was dead, sometimes I shrugged. My missing father, whom I didn't want to talk about.

But this man sitting next to me looks very much alive, his eyes—the same blue as mine—bright. We have the same hair, too, frizzy at the first sign of rain, like now. Finally my father stops, waiting for me. So I tell him what he wants to hear. But it comes out muffled.

"Good, good," he smiles. "I hate you, too."

But sitting next to my father for the first time in years, it's not hate that I feel. It's not love either, but a strange kind of remembering. Not of this father, who's wearing a half-zipped black sweatshirt and Mardi Gras beads, but the one in a herringbone coat staring up at the Manhattan sky. The blue squeeze of sky between concrete buildings. Next comes the click and whoosh of bus doors, sunlight on ice, old men in elbowless jackets lying on top of metal grates, their newspaper blankets blowing. My father has me by the hand, he's steering us clear around.

"So," he says now. "What is it you'd like to know?"

He thinks I'm a reporter. Of course. My red raincoat and new shoes. Black lace-ups I'd bought for work. I calculate property taxes, talk with homeowners in the Warren County Assessor's Office. Been there for years.

A part of me wants him to think we've never met.

"You had a good life in New York, right?" I ask, trying not to sound nervous. "A successful career at the *Times*. A family. What made you leave?" I've always wondered. What was the real reason.

"Drugs," he says, folding one knee close to his chest. "I'd have to say it was drugs." He tells me how this guy he worked nights with on the Metro Desk first got him stoned. "I stayed high for, like, three days."

"Really?" I say, turning it into a question. I know this. I've read this.

He nods. "Then I did acid. And whooooa. I realized there was more to life than just getting ahead. Working unbelievable hours. I mean, the pressure not to fuck up was intense."

His mind melted, I overheard my mother say once.

"I thought if I could get that much pleasure from a single joint, or hit, or whatever, why was I busting my ass doing all these things I didn't want to do? Fuck it." Now he tells me what nobody in my family would talk about, but is all right there in print. The hallucinogens. Dope. He says he stopped doing drugs when he moved outside because he wanted to get there naturally. "Now I'm addicted to fresh air," he says, lifting a white eyebrow. "Sun. What comes in and goes out of the park is incredible. But drugs are what got me started. I felt connected to everything."

"Everything?"

"Yes. Everything," my father says, giving me a funny look. "It was life changing."

"What about your family?"

He opens his mouth and nothing comes out. I turn to see a man in a gold helmet and boots pedaling a bicycle up the street. He's odd, even for here, dragging two spray-painted gold bins filled with crushed newspaper and aluminum behind him. "Hate!" he yells, "Fuck you!"

"Fuck you, too!" my father shouts back cheerfully. The man gets off his bike, walks over, and hands my father a smooth, white egg. The two silently touch palms. He bikes away. My father lights another cigarette as if this is nothing unusual. One eyelid crossed with tiny red veins flickers the way it always did when he smoked. "Up until that point in my life," he says, ignoring my question, "I did everything I thought I was supposed to. Got married. Cut my hair short. Worked my way up at the *Times*. I was making good money. But I'd turned into concrete. A complete shit. I had everything I thought I wanted. But I wasn't satisfied."

I stay quiet.

"So I just stopped. I quit the *Times*. Left my wife," he says without emotion. "I started defying everything I'd ever been told. Even everyday things, like looking both ways when you cross the street. That was stupid. One day I got creamed chasing a Frisbee across Eighth Avenue in New York. I smashed my thigh and was in traction for, like, three months."

"You were?" This I've never heard.

He nods. "I woke up in the hospital the next morning and couldn't speak. Not a single word."

"What happened?"

"I had a complete emotional breakdown," he says intently. "Nothing in my life was working. My marriage had ended. The *Times* refused to give me severance pay. Even words were gone. I'd always had words."

My father sighs and his lips stay open for a moment. There are no teeth behind them anymore. His gums are empty, but I don't hear a lisp.

"In the hospital, you know, I had time to think. I'd always been in a hurry before, finishing college, finding a job, writing news stories. For the first time in my life, I had a chance to really think." He lights another Virginia Slim off the one still burning. "That's when it came to me."

"What?" I ask, still hoping to hear about a daughter.

"I had to leave. As soon as my leg healed and I could talk again, I packed up and took off for San Francisco. Never went back."

"You're kidding."

"Nope," he says with satisfaction. "Never."

Liar. Of course you went back, don't you remember? I remember. You, there all night in that battered VW, the engine idling, gasoline smells seeping in the corners of our living room window. For hours I watched you, your fingers tapping the steering wheel, clicking the radio off and on, David Bowie wafting into the room, too. *Come away from that window,* my mother kept saying. *You know I can't let you near him. I can't even let that man in the house, the way he's gotten.*

My father blinks smoke out of his eyes. I sit on one hand, and the other, watching myself become the girl who never questioned her mother so at least she'd stay. Someone who can't challenge the man next to her now.

He hugs his knee closer and leans back. "You know, the park's amazing. I mean, by any sort of societal standard, I'm completely whacked. I say the *worst* things to people, *Fuck you. I hate you.* All they do is smile. *Have a lousy day!* I yell. They laugh. You probably think I'm nuts. But here in the park, I'm accepted. I've got my people. And I'm getting known in the world."

I can't listen to another word. I stand abruptly, staring down at my father's mismatched shoes. No one here—not Krash, not the man with the gold helmet, not any of the weirdoes he'd probably call *family*—knows I exist. I'm forty-seven years old and they should know I exist. A police car speeds past, its siren screaming. A second one blasts by. I can't hear what my father's saying, his lips are just moving, forming words I couldn't care less about.

I look at the watch that isn't strapped around my wrist, that isn't anywhere. "I have to go."

He squints in the sun, now directly overhead.

"I'm late," I lie. "For another appointment."

"Sure," he smiles. "Come back if you want."

When I walk away, he calls after me. "Anytime. I'm here. Just ask for Hateman."

...

What I want to do is go home. Scan numbers at work, talk to people with clean faces, check bills. I hurry down the crowded street to Telegraph Avenue and take the agonizingly slow elevator up to the third floor of my building. It's a dive, this place, filled with rent-by-the-week rooms that looked fine on the internet, a place I assumed had to be okay because it was only four blocks from the university. The walls are painted a too-bright white and the new orange carpet is already buckling. It rolls ahead of me in waves.

I unlock my door and pull the suitcase out from under the bed. Stop, I tell myself. He left a long time ago, remember. Decades. My arms ache. I call to reschedule my flight but all they can give me is something in the morning. I pay the extra fee and take it. I fold a bright red blouse in thirds—a blouse I thought my father would like, but now will never see—and roll up a pair of gray slacks. Suddenly I'm exhausted. The bed's springy and uncomfortable, but still I lie back. Then I'm gone, fast asleep I guess, because the eyes I didn't realize I had closed, open. A loud pounding is coming from below. Hammers, maybe. Or worse, an earthquake? The noise gets louder. The only window in my room looks out on the airshaft. I speed down the stairs—because who knows what might have happened to the elevator— and push the big door out.

It's night now. The clouds have cleared, but no moon shines down. Dozens of people are walking up and down the middle of Telegraph, banging things. One man beats a huge white bucket with a giant spoon, another clangs two cook pots together—pots I remember from the park. I look around for my father but he's nowhere to be seen. I stand on the sidewalk, letting people push past me. A woman leans over and lights garbage in a garbage can. A thin yellow flame shoots up.

Certain that plate glass is going to get smashed, I turn and head back to my room. This is a riot, I think. People riot all the time in Berkeley, I've heard.

The sounds change, take on a kind of rhythm. A woman laughs. I look back over my shoulder and see an old man playing his shopping cart like a xylophone. This isn't a riot. It's a party. Students, homeless, anyone, taking over the streets. The fire flickers, but doesn't flare.

A woman in a tinsel-threaded jacket hooks her arm in mine. "You can't just stand there," she says, pulling me ahead. "Come on!"

I let her take me. In Monroe, people only walk in the middle of the street during the Fourth of July parade, and noise ordinances are strictly enforced. Tomorrow I'll be back there. But tonight—the woman walks quickly and I have to hurry to keep up. The crowd folds in around us, teenagers with crew cuts, balding men with ponytails trailing down their backs, an old woman pushing a stroller filled with faded album covers. Two boys pound a gray metal parking meter as if it were a conga. The woman smiles at me, then moves on ahead.

I step in and out of circles of light from the streetlamps above, people moving all around me. I pass shadowy shop windows, dark doors. A brown-haired woman in pink curlers sits down in the street and drinks from something twisted in paper. I walk around her.

Out of a doorway, someone moves toward me with firm, slow steps. I walk faster but he matches my pace. I see a black shoe, then a white shoe comes up to meet it.

My father smiles, the corners of his eyes wrinkling. I know he's going to tell me to say *I hate you* so he can say it back. No, I decide. I'm not doing it. I'm not doing any of that hate stuff.

Without a word, my father reaches out and touches the gray in my hair. "Krash mentioned something about a woman from Monroe," he says, not calling me Toni, Smudge, anything. "Then I saw you just now. The way you tucked your chin in just like your mother—" His hand drops. "But older."

I pull away. Tonight my father's wearing a pillbox hat, an old Jackie Kennedy throwback, covered with plastic yellow daisies and pink blossoms, real ones. He's got on three sweatshirts, each collar dirtier than the next.

"Look," he says urgently, the tension building in his face. "Your mother—" His voice trails off. "I *was* turning into concrete. I had to leave. But that had nothing to do with you."

It's awful how long I wanted to hear those words.

He keeps talking, stopping only to take an immense drag on his cigarette before diving back in, explaining, justifying, an endless stream of words.

He doesn't want me to hate him, I realize. The one person in the world who should, shouldn't.

"I— I—" he's saying.

These last two words sum up everything. A roar starts building in my ears and suddenly I'm shouting, things flying out of my mouth as if they were spring-loaded and waiting. "You!" I yell. "Is there anyone else on the planet besides *you*! What about Mom, me? Or did you forget?" I'm zigzagging now all over the sidewalk, pressing forward every time he steps back. "You think you're the only person in the world who's turned into concrete? You think you know!" I see myself in the dark shop window beyond him, my arms flinging. "Years!" I shout. My reflection dips in and out of the shadowy glass, here, gone, like selves passing. "And years!" The lonely seven-year-old, shy teenager, the woman marrying, divorcing, burying her mother. All the selves he never knew. Missed entirely. "I HATE you, Dad! I mean it!" Even though my legs are kicking and elbows jabbing, it's not pure hate I feel, but an unnerving mix of love, hate, fury, and sadness. So much sadness.

"Lark," my father says. "Wow. That's incredible." I can't tell if he's smiling with some kind of fatherly pride or because he likes the new name he just gave me.

"You wanted a real conversation, Dad," I say, my voice shaking. "Here it is." This man is your father, I think. Look at him.

"I hate you, too," he says, still smiling. He touches one of the flowers on his hat as if to make sure it's still there.

My father's eyes move past mine, staring at something just over my left shoulder. His feet start shuffling together and apart, nervously.

Five or six people have gathered, how long they've been standing there, I can't tell. The sounds of pounding and pulsing are still coming from everywhere, but right around us I sense a silence. Krash's head rises above the group. The man in the gold helmet stands on one side of him. On the other is a big woman with purple-orange dreadlocks and bare feet. My father walks toward a man whose face is covered with tattoos. Chinese, maybe. The blue characters ride up and down his cheeks every time he smiles, which he's doing now, back and forth, with my father. They exchange a soft *fuck you*.

Krash comes over to me, smoking something that's definitely not a cigarette. He holds it out, but I shake my head. Everything's strange enough already.

He takes another deep drag. "You're back," he says in a tight voice, trying to hold the smoke in. His body's calm now. "You and Hate connect?"

I nod. I don't volunteer that Hateman is my father and Krash doesn't ask.

He exhales a slow stream of smoke. "Good man, Hate. Don't know what we'd do in the park without him."

Try being his daughter, I turn to say.

But Krash is gone.

A circle's formed around my father, everyone spilling off the sidewalk and into the middle of the street. My father's got this plastic pail wedged under his arm and he's drumming it, drumming hard. His elbows are out straight and his knees bending so deeply it looks as if he could fly off. Krash pulls out a splintered drumstick and starts battering a chained bicycle wheel missing its bicycle, completely off beat. The big woman twirls. I keep trying to catch my father's eye, but his face is always turned away.

OUT OF THE BOX

MYRON KAUFMAN

1986. **ELLEN AND NORMAN ARE MAKING** love in their almost-dark motel room. She's naked and her wedding dress is draped over the back of a chair. Norman is naked except for his socks.

1987. The scene is almost the same. The bedroom is now in Ellen's and Norman's Queens, NY, one-bedroom apartment. It's rainy and windy outside. Ellen is naked and Norman is wearing a different pair of socks.

1988. 1989 . . . present. The scene repeats and repeats approximately once each week. Except for the weather du jour and the color of Norman's socks. Ellen is now wearing her new *je t'aime* embroidered nightgown, pulled up to her waist. Things are more or less the same. Norman sometimes mumbles almost inaudibly, counting strokes, ". . . sixty-six, sixty-seven, sixty-eight." He stops counting and shudders. "Nowhere near one hundred and seventy-two."

Ellen sighs and, pushing gently against Norman's shoulders, dislodges him. He rolls over and they both study the ceiling.

Ellen, politely clearing her throat, starts, "Norman I've been thinking—"

Sounding irritated, he interrupts her with, "Excuse me, I've got to pee." He leaves.

Ellen straightens her gown and smoothes her hair.

Norman returns to bed and turns his back.

Ellen is embarrassed and apologetically tries again, "Norman did you ever wonder how come orthodox Jews have so many children?"

No answer.

She goes on. "The Catholics also seem to have big families. Look at the O'Neals across the street. I've lost track but they have five or six kids and how about—"

Norman suddenly sits up in bed, clearly annoyed. "All right, all right, but what does any of that have to do with us? We've been going through this same thing every week for the last fifteen years and to tell you the truth Ellen I'm sick and tired of the whole thing."

Ellen, quiet for a while, almost whispering, "It's been nineteen years . . . It's humiliating to me . . . I don't feel like a woman. All of my—"

Norman interrupts, "Look, I can't take this anymore. We've tried everything reasonable we can think of. What more can we do?"

Norman sits up with his feet on the floor and his back toward Ellen.

Ellen, waiting about ten or fifteen seconds goes on, "That's what I was trying to say. Maybe if we lived a better more spiritual life, became more religious that would help."

Norman stands up and starts pacing. "Look, I don't want any part of this. What are you talking about? We've never been religious. I don't want any part of this. I don't like going to temple."

Ellen, her voice becoming more determined. "I've made up my mind. I've made an appointment with Dr. Fleischman for tomorrow. I'm going to talk to him about our situation. I'm going to talk to him about our joining the temple, doing good deeds, volunteer work, getting more religious, becoming kosher."

Norman, now sounding defeated says quietly, "Anything but kosher."

They both become quiet. Norman gets back into bed and with their backs facing each other they close their eyes.

The alarm goes off at 7:00 a.m. and startles them both.

HUNGER

COURTNEY BIRD

1

LORNA ATE DAVID IN PIECES. SHE gnawed on his metatarsals the way you might pick at the small bones of a fish. She roasted his thigh with garlic and thyme and lemon. His right calf she carved from the shinbone and sautéed in butter. His left she rolled in breadcrumbs and baked at 400°. She kept the body in the kitchen and mopped the tile floor every night. She expected it to smell like something rotten but instead it smelled like onions and cinnamon and then, after she cleaned, like lemongrass and ammonia. She bought a new mop after three days. The freezer was full.

When his business partner called, she told the woman that David was on Ellesmere Island.

"Family emergency," she said.

She ate by the light of thirty-seven candles and played music from David's speakers on David's computer. She read through his emails and his journal. She burned pictures of his ex-girlfriends in the flames and it wasn't because she was angry or jealous. It was because she knew that she was his and he was hers and no one else was worth remembering. The last entry in his journal was a sketch of her on a swing, her shadow stretching long and waifish below. They were in love, soon to be married. Her mother thought of him as a son and his mother thought of her as a daughter. They ordered for each other at restaurants, complained about the same stop signs, laughed at the same jokes. They had sex every morning and every morning she thought it would be enough to make her happy but it never was.

And then he proposed and that, she thought, would be enough. The ring was beautiful and heavy on her finger and everyone admired it. It was a symbol that she belonged to him. And yet, she was alone inside of her small, pale body and he alone in his. She couldn't feel what he felt or see what he saw and she hated it, the way he was so separate from her.

She used the edge of her ring to open the skin along his shoulder blade. She mixed his eyelashes into salsa and ate them with chips. Hunger was a vast empty sky within her. She ate to fill it and was never full.

2

Her coworkers commented on her skin. Her cheeks were glowing. Her eyes were bright and clear, like they were holding a secret. Was she pregnant? Had she eloped? What kind of under eye cream did she use? She hadn't gained weight, but there was a pleasant fullness to her face, a blooming of something. The wrinkle between her eyebrows had flattened out, they said. She went into the bathroom and examined her face. Nothing looked different to her. Her cheekbones were still unremarkable. Her eyes were still gray and set slightly too wide. There was still the same emptiness. She missed David. The entire point was to never feel lonely, to never miss David, to keep him inside herself, to make her whole, and here she was, missing him, holding the bathroom sink to keep herself from falling.

3

Molly came over on a Wednesday with a bottle of wine. She said that Lorna had not been herself, had skipped yoga and book club and hadn't been at the coffee shop for well over a week. Outside, birds and squirrels bickered at the bird feeder. Lorna had ground up David's bones and mixed them with sunflower seeds. She cringed to think of him inside the body of a rodent, but there were so many bones to dispose of. She'd planted the larger ones under the magnolia tree in the backyard.

"I'm just tired of the distractions," Lorna said. "There's never enough time."

"Don't say *just*. Women always say *just* and it undercuts the way that you feel, as a woman. Your feelings are valid. Embrace them. Anyways, I read that in an article," Molly said.

"Don't say *anyways*. It dismisses your previous thoughts, as a woman."

"Yes, exactly. That's exactly the kind of mentality I'm talking about." Molly scratched at a stain on the counter. It came off on her thumbnail, flakey and black.

"Here, let me get that," Lorna said. She was acutely aware that Molly's back was to the freezer, that inside the freezer was a human head wrapped in three shopping bags and secured with twine. She didn't consider herself a murderer. That word was cruel and she hadn't been cruel. David had barely felt a thing. She'd done it when he was happy and deeply asleep, which she knew because she'd drugged him first and then she used the sharpest knife. She did it for both of them, because to be human is to be alone but to be in love is something different. Being one inside the other—*that* is unity, *that* is love. Still, she didn't trust Molly to understand. Molly lived with a magician and they thought that true love was a capitalist construct made to distance people from the truth.

"How long is David gone?" Molly said.

"Until they find the body, I guess."

4

The family emergency was complicated. David got a phone call from the Canadian authorities one night and the next day he was on a plane to Ellesmere Island. See, his great-great-grandfather was an archeologist studying the twelfth-century trade between Icelanders and North American Inuit. He found an armband inscribed with runes and then promptly disappeared. Cursed. The authorities found his diary and thought there might be a body nearby.

David's business partner was furious. He had missed a meeting with the governor. "The governor!" she said over the phone. "I had to sit in a conference room with the governor and talk about oil prices. I don't even believe in oil. Or the goddamn governor for that matter. Fuck David."

"Don't you work in commodities?"

"Jesus Christ. I work in gold, Lorna. It's a completely different market. People have been trading gold for thousands of years. There's history there."

"But you're partners."

"And focusing on different areas strengthens the partnership."

Lorna imagined the woman at David's desk, checking David's voicemail and watering his orchids while he was away. She imagined them in meetings together, the woman saying David's name over and over again. This is my associate, David Hadfield. Oh, David's the best in the city. David Hadfield, the most handsome oil investor at the most prestigious firm. David's not available on Tuesday, but we'd love to have lunch on Thursday. I know everything about David because we work so closely together and I know where he is at every second except right now because right now he's inside of his beautiful fiancée and their beautiful fucking freezer. Lorna had only met the woman twice and she couldn't now remember her name, but she and David were very close, Lorna knew. They would drink champagne after putting a major deal to bed and they would go running after work in the spring. Lorna never thought anything of it.

"Still, I don't think oil's something you can believe in or not believe in," Lorna said. "It exists."

"Temporarily," the woman said. "The market is in shambles. I mean, it's really hitting the shitter and it's only getting worse so you tell your fiancé that and also that he's a goddamn bastard and probably fired."

"That seems dramatic," Lorna said.

"He's lucky I'm so loyal," she said.

Lorna fingered the buttonhole on her shirt. She didn't like the sound of the woman's voice. It was deep and raspy, like she smoked cigarettes at night or studied film stars from the 1940s. Controlled and reckless and lovely all at once in a way that Lorna couldn't imagine being.

"You're not his fiancée," Lorna said. "You don't need to be loyal to him."

"Loyal in a professional sense, of course."

The woman's voice was so familiar; the way she breathed mid-sentence was so familiar. There was something sweet to it. The more she listened to the woman, the more she liked the way she breathed. If she were David, wouldn't she want a partner who breathed just like that? Yes, she would. She'd want just this kind of partner with just this kind of dark, rooted, irreverent voice. She would work until 4:00 a.m. with this kind of partner, like David did. She would come home smelling like sweat, exhausted, like David did. She wanted to hear the woman say David's name. She liked the sound of it on her tongue. David Hadfield. She imagined the woman saying his name, her breath on his neck. Lorna moved her fingers to the waistband of her pants, past it, began touching the lace of her underwear. Her fingers were warm and the woman's voice was warm and the warmth spread through her belly like something alien.

She said goodbye, to call with any more questions. She slammed the phone down on the counter. She closed her eyes and imagined the woman's face, remembered the way her dress clung to her body at the Christmas party, what a good, strong body the woman had, how her calves looked in her heels and then afterwards, when she took off her shoes to dance and her hair clung to her temples when it fell from her bun. Lorna felt the woman's fingers on her forearm, her ass, the nape of her neck. They were familiar. How? Why? Ghost traces of a hand she knew. She felt the woman's lips touch the skin behind her ear. Desire raked through her, uncontrolled, as if it belonged to someone else.

5

She slept on David's side of the bed and in the morning, she wore his slippers. She poured two teaspoons of his refrigerated blood into her coffee and packed a sandwich made with meat from his lower back. At work, she noticed that her shoes were too small. She had trouble reading, as if her eyesight had gone sour overnight. She ate the sandwich by 10:00 a.m. and became hungrier. She thought of David's business partner and how she, Lorna, went to bed exhausted and confused and empty of everything but desire for this unknown woman. It scared her. She began writing emails furiously, demonically, trying to distract herself. A bird sat on the window ledge and watched her type.

At noon, Molly came in and said, "What the fuck Lorna," and showed her an email that she'd signed with David's name.

"Wow," Lorna said, not entirely convinced it wasn't her name too. "I must really miss him."

6

Lorna had been in love before. There was Thom, who had braces on his bottom teeth, and Christopher, whose mother had cancer. They made her laugh. She envisioned certain futures with them—a garden in the bed of a truck or a sailboat christened with her name. They inspired her in little ways. Say Thom found a mushroom and quizzed her on its health benefits. Say Christopher bought her a pair of Louboutins. That kind of inspiration. She had never felt like they were the same person.

David was different. He'd been a one-night stand. Something to distract her when she was lost. He stayed the night and made French toast. He stayed the next night and made poached eggs. He brought his dogs over and Lorna became a dog person. He preached atheism and Lorna stopped going to church with her mother. On the good days, she felt like she was sixteen. In love. Found. On the bad days, she felt the weariness of the whole world in her bones. Still in love, but sadly. Still lost. He was a person with a solid, fixed heart and she was a person with a heart made of water. He'd once said, in a sweet moment, that he wanted to crawl inside her and live there, with her skin wrapped around him like a cloak. Keep warm. A solid can dissolve in a liquid, if it's willing.

7

The first thing she noticed was a hair on her left big toe. She reached for David's reading glasses and inspected it. She couldn't remember if it had always been there. She took out the tweezers but it grew back and soon there was a patch of dark fuzz on her ankles. The tights she wore to work itched. She saw women on the subway with wide-legged pants. She bought some.

At book club, Molly put her hand on Lorna's knee and leaned across her. Lorna lost her breath. Realized that Molly was an attractive woman. Realized that Molly's perfume made her feel lightheaded. She felt her heartbeat in her throat. In the bathroom, she ran her wrists under cold water and looked at herself in the mirror. Her face seemed longer. Her jawline more defined. David's glasses made her look like David. She decided not to sit next to Molly. Not to sit next to anyone. She went home and watched David's porn, found that she liked porn, imagined herself as the man. She drank hot water and blood. Dipped her finger in the blood and drew on her belly.

8

When she ran out of David, Lorna stopped eating for two days. It seemed sacrilegious to put something else in her body. It seemed like giving up on him.

9

But the body's instinct is to survive and on day three, Lorna ate a cracker. She woke up early, the way David used to, and plucked the hair off her chest. They say that when someone is severely malnourished, their skin grows hair to keep them warm. It could have been that. It could have been grief or the physical manifestation of guilt or a reaction to a soul-deep kind of cold or an overabundance of testosterone.

On the phone with her mother, Lorna began to cry. She said that David was missing, that there was a blizzard on Ellesmere Island.

"I don't know why you'd let him go up there in October," her mother said. "It's suicidal. You know, it's a woman who controls the relationship, Lorna. Maybe you should think about that."

"Coming from the expert."

"I'd rather be myself than still be married to your father," she said.

Rain fell on the bones buried beneath the magnolia tree. It fell on the birdseed in the driveway and on the squirrels sitting on their haunches with fingers raised to lips. Lorna took the drawers out of the freezer and put them outside to let the water rinse them. And then, because there was an edge of guilt in her and the desire, maybe, to drown, she took off her clothes and lay on the grass and she didn't think about whether the neighbors could see because the rain was falling so hard she could barely make out her own navel. Her skin became rough with goose bumps and her nipples hardened as the rain fell. She closed her eyes and tried to find David inside of her. She heard his voice and tasted his lips and smelled his aftershave. But she didn't feel loved. And maybe that's the way grief works, she thought. Maybe it's impossible to become someone else and now, instead, she'd lost him. A dead thing cannot love you back. She pulled at the hair on her jawbone. She stared into the falling rain and imagined being swallowed whole.

10

His business partner arrived with a box of potted orchids. She said, "I'm going on vacation for a week. I don't want these to die." The largest was a lady slipper orchid with two long, weighted branches. The flowers were maroon and soft yellow.

Lorna pointed to it. "I didn't buy him that one." Lorna and David went to the orchid show every spring. She would point out her favorites, the white and speckled pink moth orchids, and David would always agree. It used to make her smile because she knew they were alike in every way. He kept them in his office to remind him of her.

"It's not very pretty, is it?" Lorna said.

"God, no," the woman said. "It's not pretty at all. That's why I bought it for him."

The woman was slight with generous hips and thick thighs. She wore a tight gray dress with square pockets at the waist and buttons along the left side. She smiled and her lip liner was perfect. Her hair was long and thick and curly, the curls completely untamed, dark, growing in every direction like beanstalks. Lorna wanted to touch it. The woman looked at Lorna viciously, like she knew everything, like she knew how Lorna held David's dick in her mouth or how he wanted her to wear heels in bed. It was suddenly so clear, why David stayed late at work and why, when he went running in the rain, he came home smelling like bluebells, why Lorna had so wanted the woman the other night.

"Am I such a goddamn stereotype?" Lorna said. She bore her fingernails into the door-frame.

She'd thought David was perfect. God-like. She thought she would feel whole if she consumed his perfection, that she would access something bigger in both of them, the heart of the heart, the root of the root. But now, she felt him clamoring inside of her and she knew she'd been wrong. She remembered his life as if it had had been hers. She remembered this woman, the business partner, naked against the shower door, remembered the motel and the taste of her tongue and the way she wrapped her legs around his back after the rain, saw David behind the woman in the steamed mirror of the bathroom. She remembered the time he'd had sex with the business partner under his desk at work, how the phone rang and wouldn't stop and how the woman kept saying, David Hadfield is busy at the moment, like a goddamned assistant, and then pulling his dick between her warm thighs, how he felt there, ecstatic and guilty and alive. She remembered the texture of the motel sheets and the woman's smooth thigh and she knew that David had never been who she thought he was. Knew he loved the business partner because she was easy and her name was Laurie and Laurie sounded like Lorna and he wanted Lorna dirtier, sluttier, wilder, willing to be tied up, to be covered in whipped cream, to go on roller coasters, to fuck in a dressing room at the mall. Lorna knew because she knew what David knew, felt what David felt, heard what David heard, touched what David touched. She had become him and he had become her. It was what she'd wanted. She'd won.

Laurie laughed. "I don't know what you're talking about."

"Oh he told me about you," Lorna said. "He told me *all* about you."

She was angrier than she'd ever been. For the first time, she let the word murderer roll around inside her mouth but it wasn't she who was guilty, it was he. David, the murderer. David, the one who'd eaten her whole.

Lorna stepped toward the front door, put her hand into Laurie's hair, and pulled her head back. She ran a finger down Laurie's face, down her neck, between her breasts, all the way to the pockets at her waist. She leaned toward the woman and kissed her. She knew he used to do it the same slow way. Laurie squirmed, tried to pull Lorna's hand from her head, but Lorna pushed her against the doorframe and kissed her harder, tried to pry her lips open with her tongue. Laurie whimpered and Lorna tightened her grip on the woman's head and put her other hand on the curve of her ass. He loved this other woman. Loved the freedom he found in her. Fuck. Lorna felt herself falling further and further away. She wanted to hate Laurie, but David wouldn't let her. Wouldn't let her breathe, even. She'd wanted to know every single part of him, had wanted to believe it was possible to know someone more deeply than she knew herself, and now that she did, she wanted him gone. He was ugly and foreign and nothing like the person she loved. Everything, she felt, had been a mistake.

Laurie's lips softened, opened. Her tongue was salty and smooth. She wrapped her arms around Lorna's waist and pulled her closer.

"Is he really missing?" she whispered. Their lips were touching as she said it. Her eyes were wet and so close to Lorna's that Lorna could feel the wetness. She looked young and sad, like any other woman. She didn't look like a managing director. She looked like a girl.

"He's dead," Lorna said. "Now get the fuck out of my house."

11

A trembling Lorna locked the front door and the back. She collected her candles from the kitchen cabinet and arranged them along the windowsill in the upstairs bathroom. Outside, two firetrucks passed by, their sirens quiet and unlit as if they'd already been defeated. A young boy climbed on his father's shoulders to untangle a frisbee from the branches of a lone aspen and in the house next door, a woman placed her husband's hands on her waist and taught him to dance. All of this Lorna, standing on the edge of her bathtub, could see through the window, the husband spinning the woman faster and faster until their bodies blurred together.

She cut her toenails first and then her hair. She put the pieces in a wine glass on the sink and sang "Somewhere Over the Rainbow" in David's baritone, listening all the while for some trace of herself. There was the freckle on her elbow that David had so loved and made his own in loving it. There was the familiar scar on her knee, the one David said looked like a fish, puckered smooth and red against the bone. It was her scar, not his. He had never seen the rollerblades or the dock through which she'd fallen. He'd never felt the nails. She peeled the plastic cover from a new razor blade and cut along the scar's inseam, peeling a layer of skin so thin it was translucent. She began to run the bathwater and let the blood from her knee color it like a sunset. The skin tasted like iron and salt.

Slipping away inside of her body, becoming the other even now. With the edge of the razor she wrote on her left forearm in a broken, scratched script, "Lorna was here." She prayed the letters would scar, that David would see it every time he undressed and remember how he loved her.

POETRY

POETRY

MOON MAIDEN

AMY GERSTLER

My reputation soured when it was said
I'd roll in lunar dust with anyone,
that, drunk on moonshine, I'd become
unwakeable and have to sleep it off
in craters. They said my head was full
of empty blackness and dead planets'
frantic static. My loyalty to what
I loved, they all complained, waxed
and waned at whim. They claimed
I watched worlds come and go in smoke
and ash and sat, impassive. This wasn't
quite as true of me when I was young,
emitting softer, kinder light. Or so
I now insist, since I've grown old.

I Think about It

Christopher Buckley

ay ese mundo es la victoria,
es el paraiso perdido
—Neruda

Out in evening fog,
          it's the only relief
                   against four dry years . . .
like a bell in a church,
          I pull on the gray rope
                   of the sky, trying
to figure out this calculus of dust,
                   the brambles, the broom straw
of light . . .
          stars burning all this time for no one?
                        And the implications
of dusk?
          They look hopeless as well,
                   but there should be something.
Not that long ago,
          I was running around on my grandparents' farm
catching fireflies in my bare hands—
                   hands the cosmos gave me
to wave
          at assemblies of clouds,
                   at the passing infinites of air.
At my desk
          with a box of crayons and construction paper,
                       I was ready

to make something

                    from next to nothing

                              when the nun clicked
the Motorola on

          for the *Standard School Broadcast*

                                        so we might,
all preconceptions aside,

                    slipstream with whatever rose
off the glorious sea swell

               of the orchestra . . .

                                   Now I content myself
with a mocking bird,

                    his jump-cut notes from the telephone poll,
calling, like me,

          for some explanation

                         of the situation . . .
Reviewing the choices,

               I shrug my shoulders and shuffle along
leaving the guesses,

               the cart load of ironies, to whomever believes
he can make sense of them?

                    If I have a soul I should worry about,
it's the next thing to spindrift,

                    to sea salt

                              dried on the rocks . . .
Home, I sit in the kitchen,

                    keeping company with a glass of red wine—
I might as well invite

               the silence in to take a chair,

                              see which of us
remembers how hard it rained back there

                         as I ran with a newspaper
held over my head

          to the miserable jobs of my youth

                              thinking

things couldn't get any worse . . .
                                                or see who recalls the snow falling
in the Dark Ages of our History books,
                                        a courtyard by an abbey,
some beggars and back-alley heretics gathered
                                                around a small fire,
behind them
                a few bones tossed
                                        for the priests' dogs,
                                                        gleaming
on the dark stones
                like stars . . .

SUPERNOVAE

ELLEN RACHLIN

"Supernovae" originally appeared in *Granta*

Theory cannot be tangible fact
like driving on I-95 to get to a lecture
on supernovae with pictures
of white dwarfs sucking mass,
of others fusing hydrogen to their iron cores
before imploding to black.
I'm delayed behind an accident,
one car with a fender blown off,
hanging on the median, driver pacing
the thin turf of tar shoulder,
on a cell phone, mouth gaping
and closing rapidly, hands stitching,
the story part factual, part theoretical.

SPOTTED

C. DALE YOUNG

When all we saw were one or two
gigantic tentacles washed up on a beach,
how could we not spend our days imagining?

All throughout my depraved childhood,
throughout the years in which it was so easy
to enter a state of wonder, the giant squid

was so elusive people wondered if it even existed.
It was good; the giant squid was that good.
But now, in what I can no longer deny

is middle age, giant squid are everywhere.
It is as if they decided to come out of the closet
and, with each one doing so, another one decided

to do it as well. Just today, in Toyama Bay, Japan
one was sighted. The headline read
RARE GIANT SQUID SPOTTED, but honestly

these sightings are becoming so common
that to call it rare seems a bit ridiculous.
Face it, the giant squid is everywhere, has

jumped the shark, has signed with SONY
instead of an indie label, is starring in
the Real Housewives of Crustacea. A shame, really.

Now, instead of the fear and surprise we reserve
for a Moby Dick, all we can muster are questions
about how fast the giant squid swims, its skincare

regimen, what kind of diet it follows to stay trim,
the number it sang with Jimmy Fallon while playing
a xylophone: dearest giant squid, please go back into hiding...

ROUND FOR CORTICOSTEROIDS

KELLY DAVIO

Always willing to sit down, lie down, lie flatter, etc. But I am taking cortisone so I will have to get up again. —Flannery O'Connor, letter to Betty Boyd Love, 1950

The alarm pings for the next dose of cortisone,
and the pill bottle rattles excitement.
Tongue to stomach, pills fight to crawl back up,
and the high-pressure blood-nozzle
drums behind the brain. Next, the fever,
the shedding of clothes, the pink skin in winter,
every fat pore mewling with sweat.
The pill bottle rattles excitement.

Hard-heaving blood drums in the brain,
butters itself across the skull's interior.
The alarm is screwed tight for the next dose.
Then, the fever, while high-pressure blood
goes drum-beating down the brain.
The stomach rock-tumbles each pill that fights
to crawl its way up, bleeds and protests with twists
that will be calmed by no milk and no cracker.

The bloody heart keeps clapping, and pink skin
with its fat pores sings a chorus in time.
The skull's interior drags, fatty as butter,
as the pill bottle rattles excitement.
The nozzle sets loose the fever
as the stomach twits in protest, begs the body
to sit down, lie down, lie flatter, until
ping—the alarm demands the next dose.

VIEW FROM 18B

EMMA TRELLES

It is always the same constellation: the city

And its hopeful torches, a sky caped in wool and thorn.

Music of trains, music of copper wire humming fortunes.

What if the future arrived as a blade of wings

Slicing rooftops and the burned-up maples below,

Each tip pointing to somewhere I couldn't imagine?

What if the years descend as a moon, filling each glass

With cautious light? This window holds a face,

Almost detectable, a fading I am learning to endure.

This window a night I've scored for years.

It's December in California and the leaves are still

Turning. I'm alive.

The Study of Flight

Heather Altfeld

The augur has an orb full of soapflakes
and a pair of antique binoculars
pointed at the tufted nest of your past
and the impending guts of your future,

an invisible field guide to the bosh frivolity of your loves
and the noisy oscinary of your losses;
he sees the blue plaster of an egg dropped from the trees
and cracked open; you were the only thing inside.

He dowses the plum-pits you spit on the sidewalk
as a child that were swept by the rains
into the gutter, washed down the storm drain,
caught in a little marsh outside Biloxi

where they grew into spiny little trees
which are still luminous and alone
without you watching, or even knowing they were there,
the way you are now luminous and alone,

standing at the bathroom mirror plucking sad bent hairs
into the sink, the golden bobbin of your heart
stuck forever on a particular knotted thread.
The augur's lashes whirr against the glass

till the rough lake comes into view, where he will sit
in the hull of a rowboat years from now, paddling

your ashes out into the deepest part
where the lampreys wait—

everything watches; the stoic pines unblinking,
the stubborn chickadees
with that one relentless song, the baby owl
who could fit into your ghostly palm,

the inexhaustible autumn stars cragging their way into the dusk
to listen for that rowing, even the lone pea-crab on the shore
clips at the air, rasping your name. *Come back, little Piccolo!*
Come back! The oars turn, the soapflakes froth,

the lens blackens, the mallards burst into green flames
above, the lampreys smile their jawless smiles
as that can of your bones cracks open
their gray and glimmery treat.

THIS IS MANIFEST

KERRI WEBSTER

What I needed to survive was, currents
moving over my body.
Also, bourbon.
Saw a light through the trees:
serum? Lantern?
Baby, I said to the man kneeling between
my legs, there are kit foxes out there
and they hum when they learn a new thing
like ledges or stream-fording.
For years my soul was little more than an embassy.
I was lush, and then lush, and then more lush.
In all of my opening, who had I actually saved?
I was no one's bodhisattva. And so
I removed my body from the systems.
Walked the hills by night.
My blisters filled with sticky fluid.
A swan made a freakishness of its neck.
I was a woman of such secret knowledge
as you may think mad.
I don't know why, when we die,
all our skulls aren't jeweled.
My lover turned in his bed on the high hill.
Sometimes I was so enamored of sky
I felt my milk might come in.

THE DESCENT

KEVIN CRAFT

There was daylight therefore we grew eyes.
There were grasses therefore we grew lungs.

There were speeches therefore we grew an earful.
There were speeches we grew wary of.

Word-wary. Will he nill he. Circumspect.
First the thing then its preamble.

The people shall go a-walkin'.
The people shall go a-courtin' by starlight.

Therefore we grew musical: every movement
a meadowlark, every drink a drum.

Thirstier we grew tongues like swizzle sticks.
The history of ideas produced a cocktail umbrella.

Knives in the atmosphere, ice in the stone.
Therefore we grew calluses. Calluses grew lungs.

We knew a thing or two but they beat us to it.
They beat us into it. *What's the big idea* our fathers used to say.

SURGE

MIGUEL MURPHY

It's a kind of ease. As if you could
through the window self-immolate
against so much vacancy and ache, and hate
the white glare you're trapped in. Sunlight,
the filthy residue down Hollywood Blvd.
Another litany of palm trees
lining the layer, another carapace—

the black water, convex, like a dent
of self-reflections speeding to a stop—This.
This Los Angeles Without End. And
pause, staccato, glissando, pizzicato—
the gulf between us suddenly
plague and sweet music. Trafficked
interiors. Hesitant, you choke back

the worldly surge, halt-spurt. O
bright grassling! Your virulent
and slick veneer. Face. Career.
Car. Your bright dirge! From here,
the sea looks small, still, and cliché,
in the back scintillating pit
of the rearview mirror

as if the center of your own life burst.

BALM

MIGUEL MURPHY

All that's been done to you
has been done to you.
Twilight's blue urn, you leave your cellphone in it.
The wine consoles you,
and you take your pill, and all the promises black out.
There's no such thing as justice.
This is what we get, being lovers:
the stench of daylight, monotonous
as an excuse, or a litany
of excuses to remember: but he said, he said . . .
The sickness is a reminder, too.
The little dark of night is not enough.
The Nothing is a home.
I don't know how to console you.
I want to say, hold on. I am your friend.
I know, it's not enough,
the relief of being nothing, being
Night. (On the telephone, your voice breaks
because I've failed you.)
I'm the one who brought you that great bouquet
last spring, a spray
of veronica, belladonna, lilies, and stars of Bethlehem.
You were in love. Now,
you're in LA.
Look at me. Say it with me.
Pain is our black machine.

SOCIAL ELEGY

PAUL GUEST

I, too, am profoundly connected
to this person who died
way back when. I want you
to really know it. Feel it.
Later remark that your heart
begged, no more, please.
How you ignored it,
punk hunk of meat holding
in gory glamour
your certain death.
Ha! You could entertain then
thoughts of Brazil
and base jumping
and sweaty assignations
with whoever
lives in the apartment upstairs.
Imagine what it would be
to fall into nothing—
the excitement of another's oblivion.
See, I am bound
to that which erases.
To a brick wall. To the weird heat
of a strange bedroom.
Light which is not light.
Her touch will mark you,
you know it, you know it forever.
I think I mentioned
how often I weep.

And the blindness that comes,
then. I'm sure
I have shared this testimony.
It is terrifying
to unhinge my mouth, but I do.

SUBSTITUTIONARY

PAUL GUEST

In place of what I just erased, this.
In case of nor'easter, this.
In need of a dollar, this.
Instead of power walking, this.
In lieu of repayment, this.
In the valley of the shadow of, this.
When confronted, this.
In the event of wildfire, this.
If your parents ask, this.
If you have ever experienced these symptoms, this.
For faster results, this.
For external use, this.
Until, heavy and lowing, the cows come, this.
Until you find sofa in the change, this.
Since that makes no sense, this.
Before your raft sinks, this.
Over there, in the elm shade,
whatever you've been looking for, this.
Above the mantel, the clock says, this.
By the sighing stream, the trampled bank, this.
To grandma's house we go, this.
To the moon, Alice, this.
You have in your right hand, this.
This you will always want
and this you'll have
when it's night, when it's rain out,
again and again, this.
Of love, what else is left,
this.

Coda

Peter LaBerge

ST. CATHERINE OF SIENA, 2007

The conductor was the first man
I could have loved. I had just turned

thirteen, the kind of gap-toothed
that still had time to correct. That

I desired a man in my skin
still felt like slamming my tongue

into the gold confessional door
until it surrendered to red. I could not

smuggle a lie that size into my mouth.
There was only space for the ever-

protruding muscle of the tongue, the one
that, one January night, disappeared

like the ghost three kids reported
in the well at the peak of Greenwich Hill

the summer before. One night. One
small, ghosted night. I could have fit it

in my hands—it was so young,
undelivered: I told myself lies thick

as tar in my throat, until I was voiceless
and the church had extracted every cent-

worth from the mouth's sacred mine,
left layers of shale in its path. *Night*.

Evening. Still one I wished into
like that well, but not that well, some extension

of the body I thought I knew.

CHICKEN HEARTS

ROCHELLE HURT

said you loved their glum shimmer
& offered me a tray: little mauve knobs

flaunting slickness. how ready
I felt then—*oh let me grease & blacken*

your fingers, heat-lick me dumb.
two married to two others, for months

we'd lain like trimmed breasts, armless
in a made bed, our routine—nothing

more. skin learns to abide or simmer.
was it so different, you asked,

from what we refused? I couldn't
even try one heart that night. what to do

with its bright ribbon of aortic gristle
begging teeth like a taunt: *choke*

or come on & undo. on the still bed,
instead, I gifted you a bright flash

of flesh where my shirt rode up
& I left it. I left it.

but you pulled it back down.
from the dark kitchen, familiar hum

of your old fridge starting
& stopping. how could you,

I thought. toughening on the table,
those insouciant pink pouts

& a bowl of cold butter sauce
beginning to curdle.

First Fire

Sherraine Pate Williams

What was that magnetic buzz, the primal
strike, of potent shatter-flash come to kill
or cause? And how did that cracked spark, discharged
of heaven's heat, evolve exchange of flame
from fevered air? And who first dared embrace
that cardinal cinder's smoke and throbbing shine
with quick tissue and bone? And when did he,
as supple skin fused with burn, learn he held
genius in his hand? And where did he then
learn to grow the stoked smolder of this coal?
And which kiss tendered comfort to that palm,
passing this small blaze from flesh to flesh,
and seized the pain which kept this force astir?

WHAT SHE TOLD THE BABY

SHERRAINE PATE WILLIAMS

Your father? What to say. Starless skies above and Venus
out alone, the moon's rim pregnant
with vacuity. Orion's belt hiding. What
to say. That the hunter's dogs picked up
the scraps, those sloppy echoes, those slaps
of trespass. What to say. That she wasn't there? Her heaven

a horizon defiled, a studded horizontal. What to say?
That a cache of flesh drubbed to nothing
could not know? *Your father?* What?
Call pillage, scream plunder.
Under fingers, wood splintered in sharp relief, grooves
gouged rough, trading names, telling numbers. *For a Fucking
call 396-3127 Sheila is a Whore Mary sucks Cock.* How to say

she never got away. How to say
she was nowhere awhile, her eye
in the lie's sky. How to say *a table
it was a table just a table only the table
were your fathers in the dark.* But
when to say that sometimes the table
is not only a table, no matter what feast
is splayed there.
No matter who or how many takers.

First Man Hand Job

Martha Silano

Was it the fact of a name,
name of all men, man of whom

God said, after the formless, after
the empty, after the letting

and the light, it was good, the way
I am saying this man, though not

the one from which God swiped
a rib, is good, good because and not

in spite of having revealed
he'd given a hand job to the man

who drove him around in a cab,
God-given hand, who knows how

caring or not, only the fact
of an amoretto night, his skin,

each muscle, not fashioned
from a stolen bone. Lack

of iris interest, peony's pulse,
his land far off from the land

of female. No record of a garden,
a fruit, no account of having taken

a bite, of hiding, of fear. And most
of all (most of all), no shame.

NEVER

TROY JOLLIMORE

Their first kiss slashed open a world.
Their second kiss filled it with noise and light.

What if we had never met? he asked her,
and she grinned and said You mean this time around?

and he said No, never—

never, the song of the ceaseless waves tearing
themselves apart on the shore, the call

of the voiceless bird that fell into extinction
before its existence began. She pressed

her hand on his chest and felt the band
around his heart, the band by which

their migrations were traced, and said Never? That
would never have happened. And kissed him again,

a third time, sending a shiver down
through the fault line on which they lay. Never

have happened. Her fingers raking his hair.
Not one in ten thousand worlds is that sad.

NONFICTION

NON

FICT

ION

AN EXCERPT FROM

ANOTHER FINE MESS: LIFE ON TOMORROW'S MOON
POPE BROCK

forthcoming from Red Hen Press, September 12, 2017

CHAPTER 4
SHELTER

I DON'T KNOW THE PARTICULAR MOMENT when librarians threw in the towel. I don't know if they held a convention and decided, "Fuck it, we're not whispering anymore," or the yakking of the patrons overwhelmed them or what. But I haven't taken it well. I miss the old days. It's as if noise-wise we've trampled down the last fence.

It's not the world's worst problem, I realize. Fish would laugh if they could hear me complain, although they can't because thanks to sonar and the auriferous hungers of mankind parts of the ocean sound like New York City on a summer day. On land it's almost impossible now to record a full day's unbroken natural sound anywhere in the world. It's as if the 7 billion of us on the planet had formed the worst high-school band you could possibly imagine. But that's just what we are, devoted amateurs—which is to say that the noise we've been making isn't as loud as it could be.

Enter the LRAD 500X Sound Cannon. The LRAD, aka Long Range Acoustic Hailing Device, delivers precision levels of hearing loss with a signature blast—a baby crying played backwards combined with two competing sirens—that can put whole crowds flat on the ground unable to crawl away. Alternatively, a Henske Systems unit emits pulses of sound that nail all twenty-two bones of the skull "optionally preceded by legal warnings where applicable."

And so I turn with deep and honest envy to our lunar colonists as I picture them at the moment of arrival. Each in turn descends the ship's ladder and drops to the ground in a puff. Perhaps one or two shuffle about, but most simply stand transfixed by the almost Trappist silence of the moon.

Saying I envy that moment doesn't mean I could handle it. Years ago I attended a three-day yoga retreat in upstate New York. I'd never done yoga before, but it didn't look hard, or at least not competitive, so I figured, Why not? I'd been torching my system with mescaline and scotch and thought it could use a rest. But I did almost no research on the place, so I was stunned to learn on arrival that we were forbidden to speak. You could write something on a piece of paper if vitally necessary, but otherwise communication was confined to smiles. My reaction to this discovery was shock followed by panic. I'm not that social ordinarily, but the thought of being mute for seventy-two hours was like suddenly being encased in a tube. A few hours in I was wondering if I might start shouting or gibbering, uncorking a hitherto dormant pocket of mental illness. By the next morning I was sunk in resentment toward the Zen fascists running the retreat. Then I got sick. As I said, knowing nothing of what to expect, I also wasn't prepared for how limited the menu would be, most of it variations on one thing, bulgur I think, and the diet change combined with the sudden cut-off of booze, drugs and cigarettes put me flat on my cot with a swimming fever. Sick and mute. One thing, however, was clear in my mind. My body craved something and I knew what it was so I hauled myself outdoors and stumbled down the long slope to the kitchen. Several people were there preparing the next round of bulgur. I handed one of them the scrap of paper I'd brought with me. On it were the words, "Can I please have an orange?" The cook—younger than me, almost a kid—took my pencil, turned the page over, wrote and passed it back. "No," it read. The next thing I remember I was blundering down a road away from the retreat consumed with the thought that if I just walked far enough sooner or later I'd come across a place that sold fruit. By that point I wasn't sure which I wanted more, the orange itself or to say out loud, "I'd like an orange," but I never got to find out because eventually a car slid up beside me and in perfect silence I was returned Patrick McGoohan-like to the compound.

That's as close as I've ever come to living in space, and it's one more proof that I wouldn't do well there. But for those who thrive on negative virtues the moon will be fantastic. Just like the effects of Midgley's inventions, the brutality of noise will disappear. On the moon you can't hear a party horn. This makes me wonder, sentimentally I know, whether some who settle there might achieve a sort of Zen from without. Maybe, in the words of a Persian mystic, those lucky few will be able to "stop weaving and see how the pattern improves."

Now and then, I mean, once the work gets going.

So what tasks will our lunar settlers face first? Well, forward motion to start with, something we haven't seen much of in the past. Indeed, to think that man has walked on the moon is a woolly-minded view of the facts. The movements executed so far as tracked by the Huntsville, Alabama Space and Rocket Center are:

The Bunny Hop
The Side-to-Side
The Slow Motion Jog

I don't mean by this to disparage those iconic space suits from the 60s. They served wonderfully for the time and offered more style and mobility than earlier designs had led us to expect.

Yet the fact remains that these gas-pressurized models were heavy and clumsy and made shoulder surgery routine. Tomorrow's moon pioneers will wear something quite different, something along the lines of the BioSuit now in development at MIT. A "second skin" of plastics threaded with nickel and titanium, the BioSuit works on the principle of counter-pressure, which means shrink-wrapping flesh that would otherwise expand away from the bone. Add a helmet with flip-down visor, 3D cameras and digital reads and you're all set. In a BioSuit you could strap on wings and cross the moon like a heron. Or cross-country ski, which is what Harrison Schmitt, the last man on the moon, recommends. I can certainly picture that: in Maine, where I live, I often see folks breezing through the frosty woods, though they'd have to adjust their technique in space since the moon is a wilderness of holes. So if I, for example, were to trade in my wings for skis and push off—thrust, thrust, thrust—and I overshot the lip of the Aitken Basin near the South Pole, while it's true that my rate of acceleration downward would be just one-sixth that on Earth, falling eight miles would get me going at a pretty good clip, so that eventually the curious gathered at the rim would see a tiny puff of dust below caused by what's called terminal impact velocity. Posted warnings for every hole and hollow would require more than half a million signs, not likely even for sites already named for astronomers, philosophers, Julius Caesar, Michael Jackson or for the right price you:

...

Nothing Could Be Greater Than To Own Your Own Crater!™

But for colonists the slaloming will have to wait. The first thing they'll need to do is start making themselves a home—terraforming, to use the term of art, the process of turning a celestial body that's uninhabitable into one that can sustain human life. You might think that would be easy since we're demonstrated experts at reverse terraforming, and on the moon we'll be doing the same thing only backwards. It won't be that simple though. Fortunately there's lots of water. Water! Who knew? "Never predicted"—"profound discovery"—in 2009 three centuries of settled opinion exploded when those two probes hit the South Pole. Extracting the stuff won't be easy, but there it is.

Thanks to the robot vanguard, there might even be a few buildings already up. Via technology's new darling, 3D-printing, the bots themselves could crank out some "extraterrestrial housing using in situ materials" ahead of time—multi-nozzle the lunacrete, paint it, pipe it, then on to the next unit. When humans join in, construction will be more complex, but they won't do the usual things. You can't just take a jackhammer to romance and heathen mythologies and get good results. You can't drill on the moon at all. In a vacuum the heat would be so intense it would fuse the equipment. You can't blast. The debris would shoot out like a nail bomb with nothing to slow it down. Oils and hydraulic fluids won't function. Which leaves us with what? A member of the Army Corps of Engineers believes we may have to use tools from the nineteenth century, and when I spoke with Prof. Madhu Thangavelu, a designer of off-world architecture, he looked even further back. "When it comes to building and hauling," he said, "we have much to learn from the ancient Egyptians."

Remembering who did that building and hauling, I suddenly wondered if the moon of tomorrow might be built by slaves. It's an old, old story: an innocent lured by a tinkling bell of promises, then driven like a tent peg into involuntary servitude. Once you're on the moon, what's to prevent it? Come to that, what about the negative impact of isolation itself? Some psychologists fret that faced with a life of silence, exile and cunning, our colonists might slowly come unstuck. Part of this concern derives from studies in Antarctica, where remote settlers living in extreme temperatures have sometimes suffered a hormonal imbalance called T3 syndrome, aka "Going Toast." "I loved watching people fall apart," one participant recalled. "I loved falling apart myself. When I became Toasty . . . I shaved my eyebrows off. I was drinking liquid morphine with someone named Big Hand George."

To be honest, I think that sounds pretty cool. More risky on the moon though, so I guess we should try to figure out if it could happen there. Viewing the question from the vantage point of ignorance—the world's most crowded piece of property—I think not. What the worriers forget is that from the moment they arrive, settlers will be ferociously scrutinized 24/7 by millions on Earth via computers and VR links. Throw in reality TV and the rest and I have to think that lunar colonists will be the least isolated people in the history of the universe. Performance anxiety should be the concern. Or maybe not, because—think this through with me here—by then they may be so used to being watched it's simply part of life. We're well on the road now, growing used to surveillance, upping the dose, the way some in the past have ingested increasing amounts of arsenic to build up a tolerance. Rasputin did that, nibbling more and more to protect himself against poisoning (although as it turned out, he would have been better off stabbing himself once in a while). I bought a bottle of vitamins with extra iron at Rite-Aid recently, and the next day I was getting personalized ads for vitamins with extra iron on YouTube. At first I felt spooked but then weirdly peaceful. I could feel the glass being installed in my head pane by pane. *Mi cerebro es tu cerebro.* Horrifying, sure, but perhaps surrender is the only way to retain a certain spaciousness of mind.

An Offering to Yemayá

Carmella de los Angeles Guiol

En tus ojos de agua infinita
se bañan las estrellitas, mamá.
Agua de luz, agua de estrellas
Pachamama vienes del cielo.
Limpia, limpia, limpia corazón, agua brillante,
Sana, sana, sana corazón, agua bendita,
Calma, calma, calma corazón, agua del cielo, mamá.

In your infinite eyes of water
the stars are bathing, mamá.
Water of light, water of stars,
Pachamama you come from heaven.
Cleanse, cleanse, cleanse the heart, brilliant water,
Heal, heal, heal the heart, blessed water,
Calm, calm, calm the heart, heavenly water, mamá.

THERE IS A MEMORY THAT KEEPS coming back to me.

The world is asleep. My mother wakes me from my slumber, a soft shake of my little girl shoulders. My baby sister, who can't be more than a year old, sleeps in her crib by the window. My father, if he is home and not on a sailboat somewhere far away, must also be asleep in the wide bed he and my mother share, the one my sister and I will jump atop of on Saturday mornings when we get a bit older, whining for waffles.

"Where are we going?" I ask my mother as she gathers me in her arms. I am wearing my favorite green dinosaur pajamas, the ones with the feeties. The apartment is dark, and Mami is careful with every step down the carpeted stairs. We slip out the front door and she tucks me into my car seat.

"Where are we going?" I ask again.

"We're going for a drive," is all she says, strapping on her seatbelt and backing out of our quiet complex. I watch the familiar houses pass by my window. Everyone is asleep but us.

The memory is hazy, like raindrops caught in a spider web. We are driving on an empty road. Spindly trees rise on both sides. Ours are the only headlights in the darkness.

"Are we going to see the alligators?" This, I remember asking. Something about the smell in the air tells me we are in their country.

We drive deeper into the bayou. My questions fall away, leaving us with only a car engine, headlights, two breathing bodies.

Finally, when sleep has started to tug at my eyelids, Mami slides off the road and slows to a stop. A turn of the key brings roaring silence. The sudden darkness scares me.

"There she is," she whispers, pointing out the window. Through a break in the trees, I see the moon, bigger and rounder than I've ever seen before. She sits on the water, her reflection reaching toward us with long strokes of light. I'm not sure if the windows are open or closed, but I can hear the sea singing, calling me home.

I don't remember how long we sat like this, two heartbeats, swimming in moonlight and thick swamp air. But I can still taste the sweetness—the sweetness of being alone with the moon, the sea, and the woman who gave me breath.

...

My mother swam all throughout her pregnancy with me, at the university pool that she'd been going to since she was a student over a decade before. I like to think about me, swimming inside her belly like a tadpole, as she lifts each arm over her head and down the side of her body, pushing the water with cupped palms. Both of us floating, weightless.

...

"Mami, every day I pray that you'll stop drinking."

"Carmella, every day I pray that you'll give me a grandchild."

...

People come to my city from all over the world to lie on our beaches and bob in water warm as a bathtub. But I don't come here to tan, or to read a book.

On weekdays, between tutoring appointments, I cross the Rickenbacker Causeway and shimmy into my bikini in the front seat of my car. The seaweed-strewn shoreline is interrupted with scraggly stands of mangroves, and the water, dark with grass, barely moves. It is not unusual to find, tucked into the tangled tree roots, a carefully-arranged collection of fruit, coins, cake, beads, and seashells—an offering to Yemayá, Mother Whose Children are the Fish.

This beach looks nothing like the brochures; tourists never come here and the parking's free.

Wading into the bay, muddy sand squishes between my toes. No matter how far out I go, the water never reaches above my thighs. My arms and legs swim me to the bridge and back—a mile. One afternoon, a sudden storm steals my bearings, engulfing me in a world of gray.

Everywhere I've ever lived, I make daily pilgrimages to the nearest water source. When there is no swimming hole, river, or ocean to be found, I pour Epsom salts into the tub and soak my body, heavy with muscle, scar tissue, gravity.

I am rendered feather-light by the mystical marriage of hydrogen and oxygen, released from everything that makes me who I am. You can't bring anything into the water with you. Not even ghosts will follow.

...

Both of my grandmothers died at fifty-nine years old—one long before I was born and the other when I was only six.

The only grandmother who ever held me in her arms lived across the Atlantic. I was but a few years old when my father took me to Belgium to stay with her. Every morning, I watched in silent reverence as Mamita performed her daily *toilette*, a ritual in which she stood naked in front of the mirror and gently washed her beautiful, sun-weathered body with a wet cloth. Each afternoon, I kept her company at the dress shop where she worked, drawing pictures of hats and ball gowns. In the evenings, I played with my toys beneath her piano while she sat on the balcony, blowing cigarette smoke into the graying evening.

The smoking caught up to her. When I was in second grade, she had a massive operation to replace her heart and both lungs. Everything went as planned, and she survived the surgery. But that night, a nurse forgot to turn her body over, as they were supposed to do every few hours; my grandmother's lungs filled with water and she drowned, right there in her hospital bed.

You might say that my maternal grandmother drowned, too. Six hundred seventy miles of water lay between Havana and New Orleans, but the distance between her life before and after the revolution was far greater. In the States, she never celebrated another holiday or birthday. Perhaps the Gulf, with its murky shallows, was no match for the clear blue sea of her past. At fifty-nine, cancer consumed her body, and she died over a decade before my spirit was called to this earth, before I was able to know the kind of love that only a grand-mother can give.

...

"Did you swim?" my mother always asks when I come home from a trip abroad or an outdoor adventure.

Of course I did. I always do. In rock quarries or running rivers, around islands or across icy bays. With sea turtles and reef sharks in the Great Barrier Reef. Free diving for conch shells in the Bahamas banks. At the top of a two thousand–foot waterfall, with Yosemite Valley at my feet. Between rocky outcrops in the Mediterranean, like a fly caught in a wine glass. I've swum in the company of glaciers and in the warm summer bloom of biolumines-cent algae. In the nude and in a second skin of neoprene. In the belly of ancient volcanoes and alongside craggy cliffs the color of fire. On deserted sunrise beaches and at public pools during the noontime rush. In sinkholes, with manatees, beside busy highways and deep in the dark jungle.

My mother tells me stories of all the places she has swum. As a child in Varadero—the most beautiful beach there ever was, she says. This was before she was shipped off to Amer-ica, parentless and afraid, before she was taken from *la perla del Caribe*, land of skinned knees and a bucking horse named Furia. Years later, there would be other islands and more swimming—all over the Mediterranean, along the coast of Brazil, in the coral necklace that is the Florida Keys. But there is one Caribbean island she has never returned to.

...

I sit on the edge of the tub and dial my best friend's number. When she answers, she can't hear me crying over the rushing water from the faucet. She asks me what I am saying, and over and over again, I repeat the terrible words. I am done with her, I say. I am motherless.

I turn off the faucet. In the newborn silence, my wails ricochet off tiled walls. On her end of the line, my friend remains quiet; she knows the story well. Two women, two sides of the same coin. Too alike to keep the peace.

...

As a kid, bath time was always my favorite time of the day. I loved the way my mother knelt beside the tub, holding her hand under the running water to check the temperature. Just for now, I had her all to myself. While I splashed around playing with my water toys, she sifted the water like sand to make sure the hot water mixed in with the cold. She watched me lurch from one end of the tub to the other, stretching my arms and kicking my legs like I saw her do in the pool at our apartment complex.

"Time to get out," she'd say when my fingers started to pucker like prunes. "Bath time is over!"

"A little bit longer!" I'd say, disappearing below the water, blowing bubbles out of my nose.

When she finally did manage to extract me from the water and wrap a towel around me, my body leaned into her arms, loving the roughness of the fibers against my skin, her hands bringing warmth into each part of my body.

...

"Tati, my mother's drinking is getting out of hand. I think we should do an intervention."

"Carmella, if you think my cousin has a drinking problem, then I sure as hell have one, too."

...

My mother married a man of the sea. A seaman. A sailboat captain.

My father can read the skies, the waves, the stars. He knows when to tighten the jib and when to reef the mainsail. But, while my mother and I jump into the sea whenever we get the chance, he prefers to keep his feet dry, only donning his swim trunks when the keel needs to be inspected for barnacles or fishing line gets caught in the rudder.

Once, while crossing a creaky gangway, my father and I fell into the sea. I was a baby in his arms, too young to remember the feeling of toppling into murky water. Did I cry when we splashed into the cool saltwater? Or did I laugh, feeling no fear in the arms of my greatest protector?

...

"Jesus, Mami," I say, watching her open another bottle of wine. I'm home from college for winter break and this place that once felt familiar has become a shifting landscape.

"What?" she says, filling the plastic cup to the top. She drinks from the little cups my sister and I used to sip juice from when we were kids, the ones with princesses pasted on the pink and purple plastic.

"Don't you think you've had enough?"

"Oh yeah." She shoves the cork back in the bottle. "As if the French don't drink wine with every meal."

"Maybe a glass or two," I say. "Not a whole bottle."

"You think you know everything," she says, turning her back to me.

I retreat to my sister's bedroom, the one we used to share as kids. Now it's only her at home.

"She's drinking a lot," I say, sitting on my sister's bed.

"What's new?" My sister sits in her desk chair, her hair straight and long down her back; chemical treatments and fancy hair straighteners have killed her curls, and she's traded her glasses in for contact lenses. I can't get used to the woman she has become.

"How much?" I ask.

Gaby shrugs. "Every day? I don't know. At least a bottle. Maybe more."

"Shit. That's not good."

My sister looks away.

"And she barely eats anything," I continue, hoping to get my sister to agree with me, or at least say anything at all. "Maybe we should start marking the wine bottles."

"What's the point?" Gaby says, turning back toward her laptop. "She's not going to stop."

...

When we moved to Miami, my parents bought a house with an aqua-tiled pool. The house needed a lot of work, I kept hearing my parents say, but I'm pretty sure the pool was the main selling feature.

Growing up, my sister, Gaby, and I spent hours in the water, chasing each other across the length of our pool, limbs flying, water spilling over the sides onto the unfinished patio floor. Sometimes, I fastened my legs together with a hair tie so that I could practice swimming like a mermaid.

On those lucky days when our mother traded in her pressed pantsuit for a black one-piece bathing suit, we clung to her like sea anemones on a rock. She looked so different with her hair pasted to her head instead of in its usual bouffant hairstyle. We pretended she was a whale—*our* whale—and we used her as one would an inner tube or an inflatable raft. When we weren't clinging to her body, we were showing off.

"Watch me, watch me," we'd cry, somersaulting into the deep end or attempting to do six front rolls in a row.

She swam whenever she could, whenever we'd let her get away. At the beach, I'd watch from the shore as my mother's sure strokes took her toward the horizon. In the midst of children splashing in the waves and lovers entwined in the shallows, my eyes scanned the water for the tiny dot that was my mother. I panicked when I lost sight of her. What if she never came back?

...

"Papi, I think Mami has a drinking problem."

He laughs. "Your mother has always had a drinking problem."

...

I'm five, maybe six, and I'm standing beside my father in the cockpit of the Sorsa. My father is the captain of this sailboat, and we are making the trip between Rio de Janeiro and Angra dos Reis where the boat's owner has a weekend home. Behind us, Jesus Christ glows on the hillside. Before us, darkness stretches into outer space. I cannot see the place where sky and water meet, where starlit waves become the Milky Way.

Somewhere below deck, my little sister sleeps in a bunk with a cloth railing to keep her from rolling out of bed when the boat heels on its side. Soon, the city lights will fade away and I will fall asleep on the job. But for now, Papi and I watch for ships in the darkness.

"Carmella," my father says all of a sudden. "If anything happens, pull this lever."

"Like what, Papi?" I ask, my heart beginning to pound. "Like if what happens?"

My father skips a beat before responding. "In case I fall overboard. Just pull this lever and that will stop the engine."

I look out into the black night and imagine my father's body disappearing beneath the dark water. The thought makes my stomach squeeze, the way it does when I'm forced to drink milk with my breakfast.

I nod my little head. "Okay," I say. "Okay, Papi."

I understood then that water can hold you, and water can take you, too.

...

I laugh my head off when my grandfather's wife loses her balance and falls into our pool during dinner on the patio. I was only a kid. How could I have known that there was nothing funny about it? It wouldn't be until years later, when she'd answer my phone calls raving drunk at nine in the morning, that I understood the reason for her fall.

When she went, she went quickly. She'd poisoned herself for too long. They say her organs liquefied, her body returned to water.

...

I convince my mother to come with me to Virginia Key Beach one afternoon.

"We won't stay long," I promise, throwing beach towels into the backseat of the car. I throw in my own goggles and an extra pair, just in case.

At the beach, I lay down my towel and pull my hair into a tight ponytail.

"I'm going for a swim," I say to my mother as she pulls a magazine out of her bag. "You should come with me."

"No, no," she says, waving me away. "You go."

"I brought an extra pair of goggles," I say, dangling them toward her.

"Maybe later," she says, settling in on her blanket.

The coast of Florida is an extended sandbank, so swimmers have to wade out quite a bit until there's enough depth to dive. Even then, you can only get away with a shallow dive. I go for it. My knees graze the grassy seafloor and my skin tingles from the shock of cold water on sun-warmed skin. I recover from this transition of earth to sea and my arms instinctively pull at the water. My body gives in to the rhythm it knows so well: stroke-stroke-stroke-breath. As I swim, I wonder if my mother sees me from the shore, if she's watching me get smaller and smaller until I am but a dot on the horizon.

...

Gaby and I are watching a movie in the top bunk, the bed that had been mine so long ago, when my mother bursts through the door.

"You know, Carmella, I really don't appreciate the way you speak to me," she says, steadying herself with one hand on the door handle. My sister and I sit up in the bed, looking down at the woman who raised us. I swallow hard.

"I just wish you wouldn't drink so much, that's all." My eyes are fixed on hers, but her green eyes waver beneath heavy lids.

She lifts a finger and points it toward me, up on my perch. "You need to mind your own business."

When I used to sleep in this bed, I wouldn't be able to fall asleep until my mother had come and given me my goodnight kiss. Each night, I'd wait for her to lean in close so we could whisper our prayers to one another—prayers for Mami, and Papi, and Gaby, and Blanchie and Kit Kat and all the animals in the whole wide world.

My eyes begin to fill. "What if I match you—drink for drink? Then will you believe me? That you drink too much?"

I can see something in my mother's face soften. Then, she tightens her grip on the door handle and lifts her chin. Without another word, she pulls the door shut behind her.

...

No man I have ever loved has shared my need for the ocean. They respect her, but they do not wish to be like her, to become fluid.

...

"Let's swim to the buoy," I say, pointing at one of the white markers floating in the waves. I've finally convinced my mother to join me in the water.

"All the way to the buoy?"

"We'll take our time." I dive in and start swimming. I check over my shoulder to see if she's following behind me. She is.

Her strokes are measured and clean, even though it's been years since she's swam long distances. I wonder if someone watching us would be able to tell we're related by our stroke, the way a father and son share a gait, or sisters might have matching mannerisms.

Do our faces tilt at the same angle when we come up for air? Do our arms arc into the water with the same tempo? Do our feet keep the same beat as they splash through the water, keeping our bodies afloat?

...

I stand in the shallow water, fingertips grazing the surface. Around me, children splash while their parents watch from the shore, bodies folded into plastic chairs. I walk toward the center of the lake until I feel the muddy bottom drop out from beneath my feet. My body knows what to do next.

As I swim, I consider the possibility of a being growing inside my belly, foreign and yet native. I consider the jungle-dwelling sculptor whose wide hands carved and whittled my body, until the two of us melded into one. I consider the unopened pregnancy test tossed into the backseat of my car a few days ago, when I first admitted to myself that I was late. I consider having to make the same decision that my mother made twenty-five years ago, when I came along unannounced.

I have come to the lake to find comfort in the open water, but the water is clawing at my throat, threatening to pull me under. My heart beats faster and faster with each stroke until I am gasping for air, lost between two shores.

...

Over the years, I've stopped counting my mother's drinks. I try not to say anything when she orders a cold beer after a long hike instead of water. I won't buy her alcohol, but I do nothing to stop her.

It wasn't until I started dealing with anxiety that I began to understand the siren song of alcohol. During a particularly bad panic episode on my way to catch a flight, I was surprised to find myself rushing to the nearest airport bar, desperate for anything to loosen my heartbeat from its fevered drumming.

I have not held up my end of the mother-daughter bargain. I am nearing thirty and I have not given my mother a grandchild to love without condition or reservation.

My mother lives alone now; I think about her, and the bottles of wine keeping her company. I imagine her stumbling around the house in the night. She goes into the backyard to retrieve something from the shed. She trips. She falls into the pool. No one is around to hear the splash, the struggle.

One day, when I have a child of my own, will they meet this woman, the one who gifted me breath, the full moon, and the sea?

...

Last summer, my mother, sister and I pulled over on the side of US 1 and jumped into the bright blue Atlantic. We were on a trip to the Keys for my mother's birthday. Mami had just turned sixty-something and Gaby and I are nearing thirty by now. Gone are the days of bath time and mermaids. And yet.

...

How long will it be before our bodies return to the sea?

…

In the rolling waves, Gaby and I hold onto our mother like a raft. The three of us giggle when saltwater goes up our noses, and every now and then, Gaby or I break away to do a trick—an amateur synchronized swimming move, or an underwater somersault.

"Watch me, watch me," we call out to our mother. "Mami, watch me!"

Imagined Interview with One of My Loves, a Dancer

Joseph Osmundson

After "Super We" by Raja Feather Kelly

JO: Raja, would you tell everyone how we met?

RK: You know the story already.

JO: I know I do, but they don't.

RK: We met online, years ago, on one of those sites meant for putting two bodies together in the same place at the same time.

JO: Were we ever two of those bodies together at the same place at the same time?

RK: Lots of times.

JO: But were we ever two of the bodies they expected us to be?

RK: Who are they? What did they expect? You mean naked and touching?

JO: . . .

RK: Once, twice.

JO: What was it like?

RK: It was something like a cymbal crash and then it was something like hurt and then it was all leg, my leg, and all back, your back, and my teeth were everywhere.

JO: How many times have I seen you dance?

RK: I don't know.

JO: And how many times have I cried while seeing you dance?

RK: Once or more. You told me one time. I don't know if there were more.

JO: Why Feather?

RK: Because it's my name.

JO: Why else?

RK: Because of all the fragile threads leading to a central spine, solid. Because it's something delicate but strong. Because something that looks simple, pretty but mundane, gives the power to fly.

JO: You told me once that sex makes you sad.

RK: I did.

JO: But doesn't it feel good?

RK: It does, of course.

JO: But it makes you sad, even in the same moment that it feels good?

RK: Yes.

JO: Why?

RK: I don't know. Because I know the sad will come back eventually. Because it is never too far away, and because it is never too far away, it is always there.

JO: Raja, why did you have the surgery?

RK: I wanted to be beautiful, like all the other boys.

JO: Do you know that you were beautiful before?

RK: I don't know.

JO: Do you think you're beautiful now?

RK: I don't know.

JO: What do you think?

RK: The last one I had told me that I wasn't attractive. Or that he wasn't attracted to me. He said I was sexual. He said he would grow into it. He said that I was just not attractive to him right now. I slept there that night. In the morning I was gone.

JO: You didn't wear your whiteface in *SuperWE*. Why not?

RK: It wasn't right for it. I wanted to be in my own skin.

JO: When is it right for it?

RK: When I want to look pretty, when I want to look white.

JO: Are pretty and white the same?

RK: I don't know, but it feels like it most days. I can't wear that makeup out on the street, but I can wear it when I dance. When I dance, I can wear a dress, a wig, and heels. I can wear so many things that I am invisible underneath, except legs and back and teeth.

JO: Raja, when you dance do you think that you're beautiful or do you think that you're ugly?

RK: Both.

JO: You move in ways that bodies don't normally move. It looks awkward, it looks like it hurts. Does it hurt?

RK: Yes, some days, it hurts, but isn't that the point?

JO: And you're not sad when you dance?

RK: Sad doesn't come into it, really.

JO: My last boyfriend told me that he didn't like to have sex with me. I'm just not that into our sex. He said it three times. It took me two years to leave. Is beauty the same thing as sex?

RK: No. But they speak to one another. Do I really look ugly when I dance?

JO: The word I used was awkward, and there is beauty in it. Do you want to be rich?

RK: I'm American, aren't I?

JO: That's not what I mean.

RK: I want to own a house in New York with five rooms. I want to sleep in one room and have the other four rooms for my friends to sleep and eat and make work in. I want to be able to kick people out of the house. For a good reason or for no reason at all.

JO: Do you want to be famous?

RK: I'm American.

JO: Are you ever afraid?

RK: Almost always.

JO: Of what?

RK: Of failure. Of decline.

JO: Let me ask another way. Your work, your life, depends on your body being and moving in certain ways. Are you ever worried your body will fail you?

RK: Every day.

JO: How can you still live, work?

RK: By just doing.

JO: Do you think you're beautiful now?

RK: I don't know.

JO: What are you to me now?

RK: I don't know.

JO: And what am I to you?

RK: I don't know.

JO: And what did I taste like?

RK: I don't remember.

JO: You do.

RK: Something like apples or the tree that they come from.

JO: You tasted something like church or some of the people who go there. I believe that everyone I ever loved I will love forever, no matter what, and sometimes love looks like a shared glance in a bar, and sometimes love looks like two bodies together in the same place at the same time (teeth / leg / back), and sometimes love looks like a year or two of a shared bed, and sometimes love looks like a single sentence written together with no commas or semicolons (marry me?), and sometimes love looks like a mirror, and sometimes love looks as impenetrable and dark as a night upstate (no streetlight / no moon), and sometimes love looks like blood on white sheets (two drops, an inch between), and sometimes love looks as simple as watching you dance (does it hurt? how about now?), and sometimes love looks like sisterhood, and sometimes love looks like a surgeon (ripped cartilage / a narrower ridge / beautiful like the other boys), and sometimes love is nothing more than a dick, a mouth, and sometimes love will not stop fighting, and sometimes love looks like a boyfriend calling you ugly, and sometimes the next morning you'll be gone, and sometimes love looks like an outstretched hand. Do you know that I love you?

RK: I don't know. I don't know.

JO: . . .

Girl with a Gun

Rosa del Duca

WHEN MY LITTLE SISTER AND I were in grade school, we loved pretending we were secret agents, treasure hunters or runaway orphans. Some days we were survivors of some natural catastrophe. We'd race from playground to playground on our bikes, composing our own theme music—full orchestra, heavy on the strings and brass. One summer, Leila and I decided we needed to arm ourselves with water guns. We bought the cheapest we could find with our dollar-a-week allowance money—two plastic pistols—and raced home to fill them under the kitchen sink.

"Where did you get those?"

I turned around and saw that my mother had a pinch to her mouth that matched her tone.

"At the dollar store," I said, treading cautiously.

"When?"

"Just now."

"On your own?"

I rolled my eyes. "Mom, you said we could go wherever we wanted as long as we kept off the busy streets." Had we kept off the busy streets? No. But she didn't need to know that.

She adjusted her shoulders. "Well, what are you going to do with those guns?"

"Have water fights with them," Leila said.

"I don't like that."

Leila and I shared a look of exasperation. "Are you saying we can't play with them?" I asked. "'Cause these cost us two dollars."

Mom let out her angry sigh, more like a low hiss. "I just wish you would have asked me. At least keep them out of my sight. They're too realistic."

We glanced at the toys in our hands. They were ridiculously unrealistic: neon yellow and orange. As our mother stormed away, my sister mumbled, "She just doesn't get it."

I shook my head in agreement. "It's not like we're going to pretend to kill people. We're just going to shoot water. What's the harm in that?"

"Yeah, they're supposed to be fun."

We plugged the leaky guns and went outside. "Let's stand in a line and see whose goes farther," Leila said. "Or we could set up a target."

"I'm thirsty," I said, pointing the gun in my mouth and shooting out a stream of water. I liked the gushing sound it made, the tickling on my gums and tongue. I gargled, cracking Leila up, until I spit the water onto her shirt, declaring war.

...

Ten years later I was a member of the National Guard and, at the same time, a member of ROTC at Cal Poly, San Luis Obispo, where I was studying journalism. My military stint had started in the year 2000, when I was still in high school. At seventeen, the idea of earning money for college by drilling one weekend a month and fighting forest fires in the summer had sounded pretty sweet. So I'd joined the Guard. But as the war on terror unfolded, and as I grew into an adult and started to think for myself, I realized I'd made a huge mistake. I did not belong in the military. But having signed a six-year contract, there was little I could do about it.

In 2004 I was called up to serve in Operation Iraqi Freedom. Right before shipping out though, an ROTC recruiter told me I could finish college and become an officer if I signed on for a few more years in the National Guard, and if I signed up for ROTC. I saw it as a golden ticket. Time to earn my degree. Time for the wars I wanted nothing to do with to calm down. Time to buck up and own my responsibilities. So I leapt at the chance. And that is how I ended up in line at ROTC "summer camp," waiting to be handed another M16.

The Marines have this creed they memorize dedicated to the rifle. How it's their best friend and how they're useless without it. "My rifle is human, even as I, because it is my life. Thus, I will learn it as a brother. We will become part of each other." The Army isn't that fanatic about the M16, but there is a sense of reverence and ritual attached to the rifle. You must carry it a certain way, stack it a certain way, check it in and out of the armory a certain way. You must memorize its serial number. You must call it a "rifle" or a "weapon," and never, ever a "gun." It must be with you at all times, even when you're sleeping. If a drill sergeant sees you drop it they'll make you lay the rifle over the backs of your hands and do pushups until further notice.

Waiting in line outside the armory I thought about how, as a secret conscientious objector, I shouldn't like the idea of being assigned a rifle and going out to the range. I tried to work up a superior attitude. Take the amount of bullets we wasted, the land we destroyed. Atrocious. And the disturbing sensuality of being in a firing lane? Creeptown. See, there's nothing in the foxhole but you and your weapon—a weapon you cradle in your hands while you lay your cheek along its smooth, warm side. As you line up the front sight post with the shape of a human torso, you wait for your body to fall still at the end of a breath. This moment of frozen attunement is when you coax the trigger back with the soft pad of your index finger and feel the gun jolt alive. If you've done everything right, the half-person down the lane falls backwards and lies flat on the ground. You can count how many people you would have killed had the targets been flesh and blood and bone instead of rubber. My mother would have been horrified by the whole thing.

But as I stepped forward and was handed my rifle, I was excited to get back in a foxhole and see if I could shoot expert this time. I trotted out of the armory and back to formation, slipping in next to McGreer. For once he didn't ignore me, but raised his eyebrows.

"What?" I asked.

"How old is that thing?"

I turned the rifle over in my hands, noting its nicks and scrapes, how it was more gray than black. "It's beat up, that's for sure. And the handguards are different."

Kassano rejoined formation on my left. "Whoa, del Duca, let me see that."

I traded weapons with him. He and McGreer exclaimed over the serial number. Then the entire squad had to pass it around while I shoved down unease at being empty-handed, at letting my rifle stray so far from me.

"What's the big deal?" I asked Tinning.

"It's an A-1," he said. "They made them back in the 1960s."

"Good luck qualifying on this dinosaur," Nissenger crowed, handing the rifle to Persh.

"I bet this thing's seen some action," Persh said.

"Shit yeah. It's probably killed people," Hunt said, passing it off to Wild.

"I'll trade you weapons, del Duca," Wild said. "This is so badass. It should be in a museum."

"She can't trade," Kassano scoffed. "You know they write down the serial numbers next to our names, right? If we don't turn in the rifles in the exact order we got them there'll be hell to pay."

Wild gave the gun an affectionate pat goodbye before thrusting it at me.

I hesitated. I'd never thought about any of the weapons I'd held being in a war zone. I'd never pictured someone looking down their barrels, squeezing the trigger and seeing someone die. I'd assumed they were extras. I'd assumed they'd always been used for training. The assumptions of a child.

I reached out and took my rifle from Wild. Already, it felt heavier. I pictured it locked up in the dark armory at night, reliving nightmares of dense jungles and smoke and blood, recalling the hands of its wartime owner—some kid from Ohio or Texas or Alabama.

I remembered those neon, plastic water guns. Toys that at the end of the summer had been tossed in the trash, busted, never to be missed. And as the weather had turned cold and snowy Leila and I abandoned our adventure sagas in favor of art projects and wrestling matches and mock radio shows we recorded on tape with the boom box.

The gun I had now was not a toy. I couldn't throw it away. But strangely, I felt closer to my mother holding it. I felt what she'd felt a decade before—the wrongness of its shape, and a clear truth: this weapon did not belong in my hands.

TOUCH

IRA SUKRUNGRUANG

IT IS FIVE IN THE MORNING on my birthday. I am in Thailand, on my yearly family visit. Since my mother and Aunty Sue moved back to Thailand in 2004, I've come to Chiang Mai every summer to make sure my mother and aunt are safe and taken care of, to spend as much time with them as they age. I'm not a stranger here, this panhandle country where my blood runs like rivers of the earth. I first came as a boy of three, annoying the housedogs into barking frenzies. I've come for weddings and funerals. I was married here, eleven years ago, in the shadow of a looming Buddha, leaning against my Midwestern bride, Katie, a white string lacing through our hands and heads, believing, despite the heat and humidity that dampened our backs, that this would be forever. And now, I arrive after a year of stumbles—divorced and living alone.

I have been up for hours, adjusting to the eleven-hour time difference. My lower back and hip ache, a dull thrumming that radiates down my right leg. The bed is board-stiff, like most beds in Thailand, and the wooden frame creaks and cracks with my every toss and turn. Outside, the neighborhood rooster stirs the world awake, and downstairs, I hear my mother humming *Happy Birthday* while preparing coffee for the spirit home that protects the house.

I do not want to start my day. The older I get the more I am aware of time. I want to feel thirty-eight. To see if thirty-eight has made me new somehow, more enlightened, though I would not know what enlightenment feels like. On days like this one, my body feels the effects of time heavy on my joints and muscles, on my eyes that take longer to focus, on a brain that fogs. So, I stay in bed and divide my attention between a movie and book. I half-watch a film starring Tom Cruise as a Nazi soldier, dubbed in Thai, his voice full of bass and tremor, the vein on his forehead about to burst. I read *Never Let Me Go* by Kazuo Ishiguro, a futuristic love story. But the pain in my back—it's relentless. It steals my attention away from Ishiguro's prose, the uniqueness of his narrative, from Tom Cruise's vein I want to flick until it pops.

Tom Cruise is not thirty-eight. He's fifty-one. Tom Cruise does not have a bad back.

On my last night in the States, the woman I love massaged my back and then collapsed onto me, her body warm, her breath tickling my ear. We are new to each other, still exploring the physical and emotional terrain of our relationship. I think of her touch, her voice, her everything. I think of her beside me now, her leg draped over me, her breath on my neck. The early morning, the back pain, the jet lag makes it easy to imagine her warmth.

What I would give for her now—the slants of sunlight peeking through the slit of the curtains, the air conditioning buzzing above? Her hands. Her fingers. Kneading. Pressing. Her body moving in tune to mine. I was relearning the body. My body. Her body. She was teaching me touch. I was teaching her to receive. To lose herself in the tangle of us. "We are broken," she would say. And we were. The two of us had forgotten what it was like to touch with a sense of love and reciprocation. To share. To trust. To give in. To let go.

...

It was a year of touches. When I lived alone. After Katie moved out. Touch that was not tender, not loving. Filled with greed. Touch divorced of body and mind.

I needed it. Wanted it. Starved for it.

I have felt, for a long time, undesirable. This feeling has followed me for most of my life, since those grade school days when I crushed on every girl in class. I crushed easily then, crushed with an intensity that could annihilate wax off a candle, but most of my crushes were never requited. I presumed it was the Thai blood that coursed through my veins, my "yellow" skin that was like lady kryptonite. I began to believe what my mother constantly preached: "I was not like them"; them were the other boys, other men. I had heard the stereotypes. Being an Asian man in America meant you were sexless. Meant you fit the mold of "inscrutable" and "effeminate." Meant what Frank Chin theorized about Asian masculinity was somewhat true: "Our nobility is that of an efficient housewife." It did not help that I was raised by two women, though in retrospect they were the two greatest parents a boy could ask for. So I tried to be as white as possible. White was the only accepted version of being a man. White was the color of my friends and my friends' fathers. I never saw my father as a man, and I believed he suffered from being stripped of his masculinity in America. Here, he was seen as a short, pastel-wearing golfer. Here, he was half the size of other fathers, who possessed booming voices and booming bodies. My father only possessed a booming sneeze, and to prove his manhood, he'd sneeze so loudly it shook the foundations of the house.

And so I began to hate myself. A hate that stemmed from something I could not control—my skin color and what others might have thought of my skin color. Even when I was married, I never got over the weight of my ethnicity. I blamed my easy-to-please Asian demeanor as a deterrent of our relationship. If I were more manly . . . If Katie saw me work in the garage, change the oil, build a fence with my own two hands . . . If I could kick off dust from a trail ride or wrangle a steer . . .

If I could . . . If I could . . .

I sought to eradicate that notion of Asian man sexlessness. Sought to obliterate the Asian man. That slanty-eyed gook. That wing-wong, ching-chung chink. That boy who inhabited every Asian ethnic slur he had been called, every stereotype, everything that declared he was without a libido, without a sex drive.

I joined online dating sites. I presented myself as a person I wished I was. One who possessed confidence. One who craved adventure. One who might be able to fuck the socks off of you. The computer screen provided anonymity. Meeting and chatting with women took over my nights, the light of the computer in the dark rooms of the house that Katie used to occupy, my fingers rapidly tapping. At first, with some women, it was innocent letter correspondence, which sometimes progressed into sex on the page. I knew sex on the page, knew how to craft words, play with syntax and pace, knew when to quicken the heart with short monosyllabic words and how to stall a moment with a sentence that took on the cadence of slow-moving molasses. My desire to become a writer first came from my yearning to write romances. I grew up reading romances, those penny novels I secretly bought with my comic books at the used bookstore. I hoarded them, tearing off the scintillating covers of buff Caucasian men, who seduced voluptuous, corseted women. I did not want my parents to know of my secret, did not want them to know I was learning the language to woo. Language was a way to create. With words you can reshape the world. And I was reshaping who I was and who I wanted to be. On the page, I was without color. On the page, the readers of my letters could imagine whomever they wanted. Lewis Carroll wrote: "The proper definition of a man is an animal that writes letters." And sometimes I was an animal. Sometimes I ripped opened blouses and sucked and bit into flesh. Sometimes my metaphorical hand glided over curtains of skin down to the wet spaces of the body. Sometimes my metaphorical tongue tasted the sweetest of nectars. Yes, the writing was cheesy and cliché. Yes, I let the writing get the best of me, carried away with waves of language, swept up in how I made some women feel. "You made me come over and over again." "God, your words got me so wet." "We need to meet. Now."

It wasn't long before I started scheduling meetings at coffeehouses or bookstores. Many of these meet-ups were for friendly conversations and broken promises to meet again. Some were for the body and its urges. A hotel room. A bedroom. A basement. A car. Very little chatter. If any. I allowed the body to take over, to experience all the things it had never experienced because of its fidelity to one person, because of a marriage that began at the young age of twenty-five. But now that evaporated, so the body gave in. The body acted on the things it had wanted to do for years.

To fuck.

Sex was simple. How this escaped me for years, I do not know. Sex for a man, even simpler. I was a body. A selfish body. A greedy body in movement. In exertion. Touching and being touched. Touch was this chaotic echo of sound and meaning and meaninglessness. Touch was not caresses and kisses. Touch was rough and sometimes painful. Squeezes and twists. Pulling and pushing. Biting and sucking.

Touch.

Old French *tochier*, to hit.

Latin, *toccare*, to strike.

I was struck.

I struck.

Giver.

Receiver.

Touch without reciprocation. Without appreciation. The type of touch my mother warned me about. "Be careful of a white girl's touch," she'd say. I was not careful. White women touched me. Women of different shades touched me. I touched them. Touch that led to excessiveness, to the sin Buddha warned against: "Don't give way to heedlessness or to intimacy with sensual delight . . ." Touch in the erotic, neurotic, sadistic, never platonic sense. And for a time this touch quenched my desire that wasn't desire but emptiness. I existed in the seventh terrace of Dante's *Purgatorio*, this desolate land where static lives dwelled. "There, on all sides, I can see every shade / move quickly to embrace another shade, / content-they did not pause-with their brief greeting, / as ants, in their dark company, will touch / their muzzles, each to each . . ."

...

My mother sits on the cool, tiled floor, reading a newspaper, glasses perched on the tip of her nose. She wears pajamas that she's sewn from scraps of leftover fabric; they hang off of her like rags. The morning light tumbles through the curtains, and she mumbles something about the political unrest of the country and shakes her head. When she sees me ambling down the stairs, wincing with each step, she smiles and says, "Birthday boy, you're walking like an ostrich."

"A crippled ostrich."

"Back hurting?"

I nod.

"It's from the plane," she says.

"Why are Thai beds so freaking hard?"

"Why are you so soft?"

I roll my eyes.

"Come here," she says.

I do. Step by delicate step.

"Lay down," she says. "On your front."

I do. Groaning on descent.

She sits on my back and crosses her legs, the newspaper resting on the top of my head. She reads me the news of the day. Tells me Thailand is stupid. Tells me there is too much corruption in the country. Tells me stuff like this never happens in America.

"I think this country needs a hug," she says.

It's a phrase my mother has clung to since her days as a nurse, when a coworker complained of an ornery patient. "Room 503 needs a hug." I love the phrase in its simplicity. That yes, touch can melt the inner core of us. That it can steal the jadedness we possess about the world, momentarily, and give us a joy of being in a body. A hug. A hug has the capability of stilling a child in a tantrum. A hug steals the rigidness in the body, and we surrender into it. The movements of a hug: the open arms, the gathering of another human being inward. I imagine mortal enemies hugging. Arabs and Jews. North and South Koreans. Human beings have a natural inclination to cling. From the moment we emerge into the world, our first cry is not just an inhalation of our taste of air; it is a cry that demands touch, demands to be held tightly to a chest. *Hold me*, we scream. *Hug me*. We will continue to want this. Our arms are made to hold. Our bodies are made to be cradled. Humans are puzzle pieces looking for other puzzle pieces.

I need to believe this.

I hide my head in the dark of my arms. My mother's voice is muffled. She rocks back and forth, the weight of her bottom shifting to various parts of my back. Occasionally she touches the back of my head, soothes her small hand in the cushion of my hair. Occasionally, she says I'm still her baby, though much much bigger. "Your fingers used to be this small, like peppers, and now look at them. Thick sausages." Heat radiates from my back to my skull. The weight of her—only about 120 pounds—loosens tight muscles.

"You carry too much tension," she says. "Let it go."

...

My lover's touch is accompanied with voice, with a level of intimacy that delves beyond the physical. All I want to do is return her favor. To trail my finger along her back, connect one freckle to the next, feel her thudding heart when I lay my palm in the middle of her chest. Her pleasure is mine. Her sighs are mine.

"You're mine," I'd say.

"I'm yours," she'd say. "But you're mine, too."

"I'm yours," I'd say.

This touch, our touch, was a possession. We wanted to possess each other, with voracious greed, the way wild vines devour houses in the south. And it was a devouring. The way we kissed, our tongues dancing in each other's mouths, the taste of need, like a succulent peach ripe on our lips; the way we clung hard to each other and how we kept pulling each other in, as if we were trying to meld into one; the way our legs twisted and twined, serpents. We would say this need, this desire, was unhealthy. We would say we were being selfish. We would say we couldn't help it. Our lovemaking was fixing the fissures in us—we believed—these long wounds we've carried for years. With every sigh and moan, with every orgasmic release, something healed.

"I want you to use me," I said, my arms wrapped around the soft of her skin, our skins slick with sweat.

"I am," she said. "Do I want too much?"

I shook my head.

"I worry you will tire of this."

"No," I said, but the truth was I could not assure her of a future. I could not dwell in the days and months and years that had yet to present themselves. I was, for the moment, in my body. I was feeling what Buddha preached, this acceptance of the current state of things, this ability to stay rooted in the now.

It seems too perfect. I would tell my writing students that if this were a piece of fiction you would have to make believe in the unbelievable. But the haze of the year was unbelievable, a passing cloud I wandered through. Because here was this woman who suffered an exhaustive marriage, and here was this man who had lost the sense of himself. And among the things we needed from each other, despite the fear of losing ourselves again, despite the fear of giving ourselves over, was touch.

...

Meaningful touch was absent in the last three years of the marriage. It was not the fault of Katie or myself. Fault is not why good marriages fail. Not exclusive fault. No one person carries that burden. There was a time when all Katie and I did was touch. Intimately. Romantically. Lovingly. There was a time when we were ravenous for one another. But something happened. Or a lot of things happened. Or time happened, and we found ourselves suddenly distanced, and we found ourselves wanting what the other could not offer.

Our relationship never lacked for touching, however, even in its waning months; in fact, it was overly excessive. A poke. A prod. A peck. A tap. A pat. A push. A nudge. A hug. A grope. I touched and touched. Katie touched and touched. Our touches spoke very little. At night we tickled and played like children, but then we turned our backs and fell asleep, a canyon between us. We dreamt of others touching us, and us touching others, which made Katie silently cry from guilt, which made me wall up and suck down my sorrow. And then, the next day would begin, and again we would touch one another, as if we believed our wandering hands, our bodies, would wake something in us, would set fire to our relationship that had been smoldering.

For a long while, Katie and I did not give up. How could we? We loved each other. We clung to the notion that we could be saved. For fifteen years, we were all we had. So for ten weeks, in a small office building in south Tampa, we sought the counsel of a sex therapist.

The room was small and comfy, not a room I imagined a sex therapist would have. Not that I assumed there'd be charts of sexual positions or a clinical explanation of the orgasm. Not that I assumed sex toys hung on the walls, or there would be a sex swing dangling from the ceiling. No, the office was pretty nondescript in its wood paneled walls, and I found myself staring at a small framed quote across the room: "Reality is something you rise above," which irked my writer sensibilities because I hated the word "reality," which put me in an irritable mood from the very get-go, which I think I needed, that disposition for me to complain, to air out, to share, to be angry, an emotion I rarely let out.

Katie and I would sit on opposite ends of a couch, the therapist taking notes, prodding us with questions and observations.

"I notice the distance between the two of you," she said during our first session.

"I'm a big guy," I said flippantly. "I like my space."

In those sessions, Katie and I were free to say things that hurt.

"You're selfish," I said.

"You sound like an asshole," she said.

"You're spoiled."

"You're stubborn."

"I want more."

"I want less."

There was safety in that room. There was safety with that one witness to the things that bubbled inside of us. To the rest of the world, Katie and I wore the façade of the perfect couple. It was easy for us to pretend because we weren't pretending. Not really. We projected publicly what we wanted to have privately. I have no doubt that we did love each other. I believe we loved each other more during the waning years of our marriage, during those hour-long sessions with the therapist, and it was this love that kept us together longer than we should have been. It was this love that we did not want to lose because it was rare and it was special.

After every session, the therapist, this kind and patient woman, sent us home with assignments. The assignments were simple. She wanted us to experience "sensate focusing," a term derived from Masters and Johnson. Orgasm should not be the end goal of sex. One has to be in the present to enjoy the pleasures of touch, the pleasures of being alive and able to experience touch.

"Touch each other for ten minutes, lightly, gently, but do not engage in intercourse," the therapist said. "I want you to explore each other's body for you."

Katie and I were eager little students. We scheduled our assignments in our planners. "We can't forget to do our homework," we said and giggled. Each week the therapist added something new to the assignment, like kissing, like tasting. Each week we were allowed more intimacy. The therapist wanted us to carry sensate focusing into every facet of our lives. When we showered, take the time to feel the water, how it glides down the back. Feel the sting of the heat. Feel the slick of soap. Breathe in the subtle scents of clean. When we ate, do so with deliberate slowness. Enjoy food on a sensorial level. Taste every ingredient. Let the tongue learn new textures, new flavors. The therapist believed we had disconnected from touch. Especially the touch of one another. We had to become that child again, experiencing the world anew.

We did. We did with vigor.

But what happened after those ten weeks? What happened when therapy ended?

Nothing.

Nothing is the death toll of any relationship.

...

My family surprises me with an orange sponge cake and songs in Thai and English. They have set up a party outside, on the old, long canoe turned table. My mother tells me they used to paddle the canoe to school, and the twins could not bear to part with it. Now it is beautifully lacquered with a glass top; under the glass, in the hull of the boat, are mementos from their past, like their father's pipe, old farming equipment, and stuffed animals. Birthdays for my family are important, and because I'm two years closer to forty, they joke about my bad back and the abundance of gray in my hair and beard. "Like Santa Claus," Aunty Sue says.

Earlier in the day, Katie calls and wishes me a happy thirty-eighth. We talk for a bit, my mother on my shoulder telling me to tell her she misses her, Aunty Sue echoing the sentiment from across the room. They love Katie because Katie loved me and because of the history we share. Even though, my heart belongs to another, until my parents meet her, until she stands before them so they can squeeze her hand and pull her into their embrace, she is only a name, a passing thought, a ghost.

This is the power of touch. It tells us we are here. We exist.

After cake and song, I visit Wat Phra Singh to pray for a healthy new year of my life. The temple is near the center of the city, closest to the tourist culture of Chiang Mai. Wat Phra Singh remains close to my heart, a place where I always feel at peace, despite the chaos of taxis and tuk-tuks clogging the circular entrance of the temple, despite all the cheap souvenir tables, selling dragons made of rope or resin Buddhas, despite the backpackers and tourists who go in and out. In this urban setting, nature finds a way to invade. It is this fact I love, the combination of the natural and unnatural world. "Beauty exists in conjunction of everything," Buddha said. "With the things that belong and the things that do not."

Monks sit in orange robes on a raised platform along the left wall. The twins have organized *gow*, nine, monks to pray for me; *gow* is not only a number but it also means to step forward, as in *gow nah*. I am stepping forward. For the first time today, I feel thirty-eight. It is like a rebirth of sorts, a new emergence into the world.

Outside the temple is hustle and bustle and car horns and loud voices and an ever-moving life. Inside the temple is a hushed silence and the crisp click of cameras, a sense of peace and unity, like the white string that laces around the perimeters of the structure, a delicate barrier between harmony and chaos. Tourists aim their cameras at the big Buddha looming in the front, a Buddha with an abnormally large head; at the ornate European chandeliers hanging high above; at the money trees of donations from parishioners.

When the ceremony starts, I give offerings of food to statues of Buddha. The prayers begin, voices humming. The swallows in the rafters stir in sound and song, almost deafening. A hairless cat meanders out from a cluster of Buddha statues at the front of the temple, licks its paws, and stares at me. A white dog scratches a tick at one of the side entrances and shakes its coat like wet laundry.

I bow my head, letting the prayer pass through me and reverberate the heart.

A monk prepares holy water in a copper bowl, a lit candle perched at the lip, dripping yellow wax. When done, he whisks the water onto me and my family. I close my eyes. My hands pressed tight. The water wets my hair and back, seeps through my shirt, like the cool of a summer rain. And though I do not believe in such things, when I rise from the temple floor the pain in my back is gone, and in that spot is a strange warmth, as if from a hand.

Baby Dolls

Jennifer Maritza McCauley

MY BROTHER IS LITTLE, BLACK-SKINNED AND sleeping deep in a cloud-colored bassinet. I am also little and black, but longer-limbed, four years old with plaits greased tight by Mami's yellow fingers. It is mid-September but the living room growls with fanged heat. Mami is downstairs soaking pigeon peas and Abuela is with me, laughing at *luchadores* on television. The wrestlers glow with sweat and slippery oil; they twist, curl and snap in grotesque shapes. Abuela sips Coors and rocks Timmy idly. I watch my brother's slitted eyes, his waxy, fat-pocked skin. He looks doll-like but his humped belly is real and trembles under duck-print cotton. Mami has told me, *Don't pick him up; he's not a toy,* but I know this already. I know my brother is not a doll; he is a plushy seed that will bloom into my first real friend.

...

I am little, black and smiling, in the corner of my nursery school's playroom. It is the end of the day and I build a Lincoln Log cabin alone. The girls and boys, all pink-colored, except for Kuja and Yi, are in friend-clusters, playing with T-Rexes or Raggedy Annes or floppy ballerinas. Mami arrives early. She scans the playroom, walks about and inspects the doll-faces—the blue-eyed plastic babies with peach-fuzz hair, the princesses with pinched-in waists. She looks at me and sees me: smiling, black, friendless. Mami's eyes get red and she licks her lips. She isn't happy and says so. Mami is not black, but she reads books every day on How to Raise a Black Child by Very Smart Black Scholars and she knows her black daughter should have the right dolls. Mami confronts Miss O'Donnell then, who is laughing with pig-tailed brunettes. Mami asks about the dolls first. She points at the toys, then Kuja and Yi, then me. Mami talks loud. Miss O'Donnell sighs and says we don't have that kind of budget to change things for three girls. The teacher does not know Daddy is an Important Black Man, and Mami names all the Important Men Daddy knows. The teacher blinks too many times; she is shrinking. Mami grabs my hand and we are gone.

The next week, new dolls come to my school. They are copper-faced like Kuja and oval-eyed like Yi and black like my father, with Daddy's wooly hair. When Mami comes to fetch me, she looks to see how things have changed. She sees me: little, black, alone, and smiling in the corner, dreaming up adventures with different-colored dolls. Mami's face muscles get weak. She picks me up, and marches past the nursery school teacher. The nursery school teacher smirks when we leave.

In the car, Mami buckles me in. She sits in the driver's seat and slams her head against the car wheel. She is sobbing.

...

My brother is little, black, and still sleeping deep, while Mami finishes the *gondules* downstairs. Abuela doesn't like the *luchadores* show anymore and she switches to *telenovelas*. She opens another can of Coors, or "Special Soda," the kind of drink Daddy says I cannot have. I ask Abuela what she is drinking. Abuela snickers, hands me the can and says, "Try." I sip small, and my mouth burns fast. I shove the can back in Abuela's hands and run to the bathroom. I spit in the sink. My teeth are hot; my gums prickle. I wonder if Abuela wants to poison me. I know she does not like me as much as the other grandchildren. When Mami takes me to her house, the photographs of me, Daddy and Timmy are tucked behind the white grandchildren on her mantel. When Mami yells at my grandmother about this, Abuela always says, "It's just for presentations."

I am done spitting and I go to sit next to Abuela on the couch. I shiver, wondering how long it will take for me to die. Abuela is laughing at my eyes, then she laughs at a white Spanish-speaking woman on the screen. I stand back up and look at my little brother, whose sweet face makes me better-feeling. I tell him I love him, just in case I won't be alive for much longer. My brother stares at me as if he knows me very well.

Abuela sees me and says, "Want to pick your brother up?" I tell her, Mami says *not to*, and Abuela says, "Go ahead. It will be cute." I look at Timmy and decide I will hug him one last time before Abuela's poison kicks in. I reach to lift my brother. Timmy is too heavy for my little girl arms. The bassinet lurches to the left. Abuela cries out and catches it; I am holding my brother who has tipped over, face first, his stomach smashed against the rim of the carriage. He is wailing and I am holding his chest. I cry too and Abuela is cussing and Mami shows up. She is horrified. Mami rushes forward and pries Timmy from my hands while Abuela holds the bassinet in place. I wave my hands, trying to help, but Mami shouts, "Go!" I run away, and hear Abuela say, *I told her not to, said he's not a baby doll*, and I think: *I know!*

In my room, on my little girl bed, I press my face against the pillow and cry. I wonder how long it will take to die from the Special Soda. I think I'll never see my brother again now, and my Mami, who probably doesn't love me anymore, thinks I have tried to hurt Baby Timmy. I won't play with him again, ever. If I survive the Special Soda, I will always be alone.

After the pillow gets damp for my little girl snot and tears, I look up. I see my dolls. They crowd my plaid comforter; they are the friends Mami bought for me so I will not be lonely when the white girls say things like, "Don't touch my toys; Mom says they'll get dirty if you do." I look at these purchased friends: plastic cocoa girls with puffy braids, brown babies with wild hair, Latina-looking Barbies with ochre legs and wet black eyes. They stare at me, coldly. They are me-colored, dead-eyed, unreal.

Nylon Stockings

A collaborative essay by Brenda Miller and Lee Gulyas

DUE TO A NYLON SHORTAGE, WOMEN painted on stockings during wartime. The absurd lengths we go to for the sake of glamour. Corsets and brassieres—foundations, they were called—seem restrictive in retrospect, along with that Victorian ideal of fragility as the pinnacle of ladylike behavior. But once we abandoned those undergarments, we were expected to master control from within.

Is your body out of fashion? Should you have lived during the Renaissance, where your curves would be lauded? And those ankles? Are they slender enough? That thigh gap, your eyebrows. Bee venom masks and botox. Belladonna eye drops to enlarge pupils, x-rays for hair removal, lead and arsenic to smooth and refine your complexion. I did have a serious flirtation with expensive Italian hair dye in the '80s, my very short bright yellow hair that matched, exactly, my motorcycle helmet. Then a fire-red, purchased in cash from a hairdresser via her alley door.

But I didn't wield the bleach and dye and piercings and makeup in the pursuit of beauty. Maybe it was like that Far Side comic, "Nature's Way of Saying Do Not Touch." An exertion of power, a way to control how I moved in the world.

And what's interesting, if we gaze at that photo long enough: they are creating the marks, the seams, that normally we'd want to eliminate. After nylon stockings went out of fashion we got seamless pantyhose, in colors like "Nude" or "Barely There," to simulate the idea of wearing nothing at all. These stockings are meant to create the illusion that our bare legs are perfect: no blemishes, no scars, and certainly not a hair in sight.

But in this photo, in this time of deprivation and sacrifice, the aesthetic of beauty included the *seam*, proof that you could afford to create illusion. Men were supposed to follow the line straight from ankle to the point where the leg disappears into that mysterious realm beneath the skirt. The seam made an arrow, pointing to the object of desire.

These women: they intrigue me; they're having way too good a time. They're wearing absurdly high heels indoors, and the one with marker in hand—her bodice is a bit askew, revealing her lacy foundation. She fixes her gaze on her friend's upper thigh. I imagine the pen must have tickled as the tip drew up and up, teasing along that sensitive point where leg becomes something else altogether. I'd like to imagine they never made it out of the apartment that night, yielding instead to each other, scarcity turned to abundance.

PEARS

COREY GINSBERG

WITHOUT FAIL, EACH YEAR DURING THE holidays, someone sends the Ginsbergs the gift of food. When the token Harry & David box arrives at our house, we all get excited. One year there was chocolate cake in the box. Whoever sent that cake clearly knew my family. We stood and ate it with our fingers before it could be plated. Then we fought over who had the most. The box I'm carrying in from the porch could contain more cake. Or nuts, or truffles, or an artisanal cheese spread with gourmet crackers.

The occasion when the chocolate cake came many years ago created a dangerous expectation cycle. Since then, it's never been cake or anything remotely cake-like. Year after year after year, the box is full of pears. Fucking pears.

"Shit," my mom says when she opens the lid to reveal rows of foil-covered fruit. "What the hell are we gonna do with all of these?"

I shut the box and place it on top of the other box of pears that arrived a few days ago. This isn't the first time two boxes of pears have arrived in the same week, days before Christmas.

We are not pear people. Nothing about us could ever project a desire for copious amounts of pears. Pears are the asshole of the fruit kingdom. They get stuck in your smile, create a film in your mouth, and pass through your colon like insoluble fiber lightning. Pears are the Monday of fruit; they disappoint by design. They rank lower on the exciting fruit scale than papayas or Granny Smith apples. They couldn't be berries, grapes or mangoes if they tried. Even when they come individually wrapped in a fancy box, there's no disguising the fact that they are shitty, awful pears.

Even if pears were a desirable fruit, the window in which to consume them is so slim it's a losing battle. Pears remain unripe for weeks, like sour, green grenades. Then they're tender and juicy for a day or two before they begin the inevitable bruising, rotting and seeping process. They take up counter space in the kitchen and stare at us as we walk past the fruit bowl toward the snack cabinet. They make us feel guilty when we select Nilla Wafers, Cheez-Its, or peanut butter and a spoon. *Someone should eat those pears*, we say, knowing how expensive they were and how wrong it is to waste food. Usually my mom pawns one or two off on my dad to take to work with his lunch. But after a few days, he protests and resorts to the

M&M stash in his office drawer. Too much of a good thing can be a problem, but too much of a bad, expensive thing is worse.

This year, I have a different plan. I select a few pears from the riper box. I peel and cube them, and toss them in the blender. I throw in ice, a generous glug of tequila and a splash of orange juice.

"Who wants a margarita?" I ask as I carry the first round of drinks into the family room. If we won't eat the pears, someone in the Ginsberg family will surely drink them.

PSEUDOSEIZURE

CLAYTON DALTON

Go up to Gilead and obtain balm, O virgin daughter of Egypt!

In vain they have multiplied remedies;

There is no healing for you.

A NEW PATIENT HAS BEEN ADMITTED to our service on the medical floor. She is being transferred from the psychiatry unit after seizing in the common room, and there is talk of something known as pseudoseizure.

The etiology of a seizure belongs to one of two categories: epileptic or non-epileptic. An epileptic seizure begins when something—a physical or chemical abnormality—alters the subtle balance between excitation and inhibition that governs our several billion neurons. The balance tips too far toward excitement, and whole communities of neurons succumb to a rash carousal in synchrony. The outward manifestation depends on what neighborhoods of neurons are involved. In the case of a complete *grand mal* seizure, all of them are.

During a non-epileptic seizure, there is no abnormal neuronal correlate to the patient's physical symptoms. Several rare disorders fall into this category, but the most common manifestation is a phenomenon known as psychogenic seizure. Colloquially these are called pseudoseizures, and they have a strong association with psychiatric illness. The cause is almost entirely obscure, but conversion disorder is thought to be an instructive parallel—an affliction which may strike a patient blind or lame in the face of some terrible stressor, though the neurological hardware remains intact. The psychological stress is so profound that the mind seems to transform it into a physical symptom like an emergency sluice on a dam.

A psychogenic seizure may be every bit as violent as its epileptic counterpart, but an electro-encephalogram, which measures neuronal activity, will defy the riotous display by rendering the steady quiet thrum of normal neurons. Despite the unruly commotion you will find nary a wayward neuron's discharge. The discrepancy is unsettling, as would be any departure of trusted instrumentation from direct experience. I am reminded of the old legends of aviation, of pilots holding a perfect stable bearing on the horizon, staring wide-eyed as their gauges spin like tops over Bermuda.

The difficulty in differentiating psychogenic from epileptic seizures is that an encephalogram must be obtained as the convulsions are occurring, yet the equipment required is elaborate and cumbersome to deploy. The danger in being unable to do so is that the treatment of an epileptic seizure involves powerful, potentially dangerous medications. For psychogenic seizure, no acute treatment exists.

A final consideration is that for many, the prefix "pseudo" connotes a sham or fake. But a psychogenic seizure, as with conversion disorder, is beyond the patient's conscious control and must not be regarded as factitious. Nevertheless, today some of the staff are whispering that there are fake seizures to be seen on the ward.

...

As I near the patient's room the tech assigned to provide one-to-one observation gives me an eye from her blue plastic chair as she leans back against the tile wall of the hallway and crosses her forearms. I enter the room and pull a chair to the patient's bedside.

Good morning, I say.

Hi, she says in a soft voice.

She is tall, with a powerful build, and her knees are drawn up at short angles to allow the bed to accommodate her length. Her face is simple and full, with thin eyebrows held high in an innocuous expression, almost childlike.

Before I can speak again her expression breaks. Eyebrows screw down to crowd her cheek-bones, the forehead corrugates, and old creases in the skin are lifted up to show her age, which I know from the chart is forty-two years.

I'm scared, she says.

Please help me.

I keep my voice calm as I explain that we are giving her medicine to stop her seizures.

We're going to take care of you here, you're safe.

What is that you're putting in me, she asks apprehensively, gesturing with a long index to the bag of normal saline hung on the rack above her.

This is just fluid, I say, like water. To make sure you don't get dehydrated.

And this one here—lifting the miniature pouch of levetiracetam slung above the saline—is a seizure medicine. I show her how the plastic tubing winds from the drip chamber to join the primary line.

She nods meekly, her face a strange meld of insouciance and fear.

I smile and press her hand. She begins to reciprocate with a little half-sided lifting of the corner of her mouth but then drops it abruptly. Her thin eyebrows rise up and a mask of dread looms on her face. I wait for speech but none comes. Aura, I think—a premonition associated with seizure or migraine.

Oh, she moans barely, as a tremor in her hand picks up and her right leg begins to rattle against the metal railing of the bed. Her eyes go down to watch the macabre display of her mutinous limb, then return to fasten on mine in a wordless plea. Her jaw begins to loosen at its hinge and hang.

There is an indescribable brightness of the eye, a composure or poise in the muscular pulleys of the organ which marks the intelligence of the highest vertebrates. To witness that scintillation fade before you like a dimming coil is truly uncanny. Often it heralds the coming on of death, but here it marks the onset of seizure. I see the pulleys slacken as her hold on my hand gets loose. The brightness wanes as the seat of intelligence withdraws into the calamity of a private tempest. The quivering twitch of her rightward extremities spreads crosswise and amplifies, entering the tips of her digits like a crown fire. The heavy cranium begins to roll and saliva spumes at the lips. Her eyes tip back and become white. A seizure has begun.

My chair grates backwards on the linoleum floor as I stand and exit the room to find the nurse in the corridor.

Does this patient have a standing order for Ativan? She's seizing now—

The nurse's expression sets and she cocks her left eyebrow just so, like she knows something.

Neurology saw her already—they said she's faking.

You think that's fake? I ask with incredulity. Have you seen her?

I turn away and leave to find the attending. Isolated seizures can result in cuts or fractures or nipped tongues, but seizures which recur rapidly, piggybacking on one another, or which last longer than five minutes can cause brain injury or death and are a medical emergency. These kind of intractable seizures are known as status epilepticus. I find the attending physician and brief her.

When we arrive at the bedside the patient is no longer seizing and appears to be asleep or unconscious. The attending steps forward and leans in.

Ma'am? Can you hear me?

The patient stirs and cracks her eyes. Her mind is visibly slowed as it digests the strange faces above her.

Do you know where you are?

The pallor of confusion clears abruptly from her face as though snapped from a reverie.

Where's my money? she says, with a note of panic.

I have to pay the TV now it was just here on the table but now it's gone I don't know where it went have you seen it?

You had a seizure, the attending says in a low tone, and you're a little confused now. It's not unusual for this to happen after a seizure, don't worry. We're here to take care of you.
Oh, murmurs the patient, okay, sounding noncommittal and hesitant, like she doesn't comprehend the words.

Lie back and try to relax, I'm just going to examine you.

The attending pulls her stethoscope from a coat pocket and hooks its bicuspid end into her ears. The loose end shimmies as she leans down to unfasten the hospital gown and expose the woman's chest. She looks over her shoulder at a resident, who acknowledges the tacit request and yanks the curtains around the bed with a metallic screech. The fabric renders a gentle intumescence around the group of residents huddled bedside. The attending fetches up the leaden bell of the stethoscope and presses it firmly to the patient's skin, aside the sternum and above the breast. She closes her eyes to listen. She doesn't notice the subtle return of a tremor to the tips of the patient's fingers, but her eyes snap open when she feels the abdomen begin to tighten and jerk. She rights herself abruptly, the stethoscope freely swinging from her ears.

The first convulsion flexes the patient at the hips, arching her spine and bringing her torso up and forward off the bed. The neck is supple and her head hangs loosely from its root as she heaves. This seizure has a different character than the one I witnessed before—the patient's limbs and torso now writhe like a lissome flag in the breeze, or an eel. Gone are the staccato tics and jerks; this motion is almost entrancing, graceful if it weren't kin to such human suffering. The patient's head whips back and forth, left to right, restlessly.

The attending looks on in silence as a resident reaches around to cradle the patient's head and prevent it from knocking against the bedside.

Call ICU, she says. She's been doing this all night through the Keppra?

The resident nods his head.

She could go into status and we can't protect her airway. She needs to go upstairs. Call neuro, too, and give Ativan.

Another resident dips out from under the curtain and plucks an old landline from its cradle by the door. The long helix of the cord follows him and hugs the jamb as he steps out into the corridor. The rest of us stand by as the seizure runs its course and begins to wane. We have given Ativan, a benzodiazepine, which augments the inhibitory apparatus of the brain to bridle a seizure and break it. The amplitude of her pitching steadily diminishes until the last contracture finally expires, her body now limp and bereft on the bed, depleted from the exertion. Her eyes lie closed in a feverish sleep; on her forehead tiny globes of sweat catch the light of the overhead fluorescents. The room is silent save for the soft call of the telemetry monitor, the placid tone of its tempo filling the room like a warm medium and spilling out into the corridor to join tones from other patients, echoing up and down the ward like toadsong.

The team loiters back from the patient's bedside as we wait for the ICU and neurology teams to arrive. Two of the residents murmur between themselves, forearms crossed and heads nearly touching. The attending is quiet and broods by herself in a corner. She regards the patient warily, her eyes unfocused and pensive. There is another patient in this room, in a bed by the window and hidden from our view by a curtain. She is not under the care of my team, and I know only that she is demented. Sometime during the chaos of the last seizure she struck up with the rhythm of some inscrutable hymn. Now it carries over into the stillness like the incantation of a shaman.

Psychogenic seizure can be a convincing mimic of epilepsy, but sometimes there are subtle differences. Epilepsy often leaves patients confused after their convulsions subside, whereas psychogenic seizures rarely do. Certain movements, such as a side-to-side jerking of the head or arching of the back, are suggestive of a psychogenic origin. Epileptic seizures often leave the eyes open, whereas non-epileptic seizures tend to close them. But none of these clinical signs are consistent or reliable. Only an electroencephalogram can differentiate the two, and at the moment our priority is protecting her brain from the specter of status epilepticus.

I look up from my place against the wall and am surprised to see the ICU fellow silhouetted in the doorway, wordless. This man has an interesting history. He is Jordanian, and there he was born, raised, educated, and trained in critical care medicine. He immigrated to the United States, where he was required to repeat his residency and fellowship in order to practice. He has an angular face with a short neat goatee and closely cropped hair. His expression is a cast of immutable sangfroid, which rarely budges from its cool repose except to lift an eyebrow or speak. He carries with him the stoicism of a man resigned to the long savagery of medical training that foreign physicians often endure to practice in this country. He sweeps silently to the attending's corner and they converse in muted tones.

As they look on the patient begins to seize again. The Jordanian realigns the tall wires of his frame from the corner to the bedside and asks how much Ativan the patient has had.

Two milligrams.

Give two more.

On its way, says a nurse.

Hurry up—and get anesthesiology down here. She may need to be intubated.

The patient's eyes are now fastened tight. The Jordanian reaches over to pry one open, revealing a thin hook of iris way up under the lid. He rests his other hand flat on her abdomen.

Where's the Ativan?

Pushing it now, says the nurse as he locks a plastic syringe to the head of the IV and drives the plunger down. I hold the patient's ankles to prevent her spastic jerks from tearing the IV from its vein. We wait for the drug to work its effect. Thirty seconds, a minute. Two minutes.

Push another two, says the Jordanian.

The nurse screws a new syringe to the IV and sends more drug down the line. The muscular tonus eases slightly as the benzodiazepine saturates the blood and begins to penetrate the diaphanous membrane which shelters the brain. What a marvel, this medicine, this manmade cluster of atoms which will home to its niche like a pigeon amongst the myriad crevices and cul-de-sacs of the body, the magnitude and diversity of which must rival the very stars of our own galaxy.

The Jordanian pries an eyelid.

She's still going, by the way, he says. She's had six? Do another two.

The nurse obliges.

She's HIV—watch the sharps, says a resident.
How's the breathing?

She's satting a hundred, I say, maintaining my hold on her legs. The ankle is less common for intravenous access, but this patient's veins are sclerotic and fibrosed from years of drug abuse. Gone are the supple channels which yield to the fine bevel of the needle and its overlying catheter. Now tight little pipes bound taut with scar, stiff as wires. They flee the probing steel under a thin veneer of skin. The Jordanian eyes the tenuous IV and orders a resident to thread another line into the opposite ankle.

For this patient the line is precious and must be protected. Mounds of plastic tape struggle against a slow and steady ooze of blood to bind it to the ankle. I touch my latexed finger to the seepage coalescing at the edges of the tape and whisk the coagulating blood in circles between my forefinger and thumb. I think of the tiny virus it carries, just an ignorant clump of protein which unchecked will destroy a human completely.

The neurologist has arrived, a large bear of a man with huge fists. One of them grasps a reflex hammer, holding it simply as a child holds a utensil. The blue rubber head of the hammer emerges from his fist like a triangular bloom.

The Jordanian lifts the lid of the patient's left eye, revealing a persistent deviation which the benzodiazepines appear not to have fazed.

She's still going, by the way, he says, looking up first at the neurologist, then from eye to eye around the room. It is apparent that he thinks this an epileptic seizure.

The neurologist looks on, head canted and eyebrows high, nodding in a slow and pensive way. He holds his little hammer across his chest. At this moment I notice the twisted odor of stool. The patient has been incontinent, which is much more common in epileptic seizures. But Ativan will usually abort an epileptic seizure—it is patients with psychogenic seizures who often receive large doses of benzodiazepines to little effect.

The anesthesiologist now enters from the corridor, a slow trundling creature of turtlish countenance lugging a black rolling case of equipment behind him. He is clad in faded green scrubs with a plunging neckline. His face is a profuse layercake of fine wrinkles, his eyes a perpetual squint from the weight of the skin above. When he is not speaking his bottom lip puckers open and hangs like a jowl.

With a nod from the Jordanian the anesthesiologist steps to the head of the bed and cracks his case, withdrawing two vials of an opaque white emulsion and the gleaming scythe of a laryngoscope. Each vial contains a hundred milligrams of the sedative propofol. He passes one vial to the resident manning the IV and instructs him to draw the thick mash up into a syringe. The resident eases a wide needle through the rubbered orifice which caps the vial and upends the mated pair. He releases the glass from between two fingers and transfers his hand to the girth of the syringe to steady it as he pulls hard on the plunger. The little cylinder gyrates and wobbles freely. Once drawn he extracts the needle and pitches the empty glass into the trash bin. He fixes the syringe to the IV and with a nod from the anesthesiologist hammers down to expel the first bolus of sedative. I watch it course whitely through the line.

The Jordanian waits a moment before peering again under the soft cloak of the eye.

Blood pressure? he says, hooking his head at a right angle over his left shoulder to scan the vitals monitor. The green glyphs of the display read 110/77.

Good, blood pressure can handle propofol, he says. Push the second bolus. The plastic line goes whitely again.

The final muscular coda which has bound the patient tightly since her last convulsive ictus finally subsides, persuaded by the heady puissance of the cocktail we have fed into her veins. The deviant eye comes down from its roost at last but remains dull and devoid of conscious spark, expected under such sedation.

The anesthesiologist brushes the spine of lashes above the right eye and elicits no reflex, signaling sufficient benumbing to intubate. With a dexterity incongruent with his demeanor he expertly rolls the head back on its axis, bringing the chin upward and back to open the airway. He scissors his fingers and places one each on the upper and lower rows of molars just inside the crack of the mouth. Gently he pries the jaws open and slides in the blade of the laryngoscope, sweeping the tongue to the side and dropping down the shaft of the esophagus. He probes for a moment until the tip of the cool shank rests softly in a pouch of tissue at the base of the epiglottis, then cantilevers his arm outward to throw wide the airway. What strange taction must this be were she sensate, a cold ingot stuck like a bead in her gullet.

With the airway exposed the anesthesiologist crouches a bit to peer into the dark hollow and visualize the labial crease of the vocal cords. His right hand unscissors and leaves the jaw. A nurse places an endotracheal tube into the upturned palm. Without taking his eyes off the cords he threads the tube below the suspended epiglottis and through the confines of the voicebox into the keep of the lungs. He whips the laryngoscope out expertly and fastens a small blue bellows to the end of the tube. He gives a two fisted squeeze and nods at the rise of the chest. He hands the bellows to a nurse and steps back. A resident listens with a stethoscope to confirm the correct placement.

Suddenly the patient snaps forward on the bed and kicks her legs, wrenching the tube and its bellows from the nurse's grip and threatening the dual IVs that tether her ankles.

Jesus! someone erupts.

One of the residents pulls her bedward by the shoulders and I grab her legs again to prevent another kick from shearing the IV catheters right out of her skin.

Get some restraints! barks the neurologist over his shoulder, the little hammer still clutched in a fist which now lies heavily on the patient's chest.

What the fuck just happened? says a resident.

She is not sufficiently sedated, murmurs the Jordanian coolly. She has come through the hypnotic very quickly.

I've never seen anyone go through eighty of propofol like that, says the neurologist, and with Ativan.

Give her two more of Ativan, says the Jordanian. And get some midazolam.

More drugs purl down the thin pipe of the IV.

The patient bucks her arm up to tear at the tube and makes a terrible sickly moan, agurgle with foam and muted by an unsettling plastic resonance from the tube abutting her cords.

We must paralyze her, urges the anesthesiologist, offering a ready, drawn syringe of rocuronium.

No! snaps the neurologist. She's not sedated—we cannot paralyze if she's conscious!

The demented woman across the curtain has begun again her eldritch invocation in response to the new commotion.

Where is the midaz? asks the Jordanian.

It's here, says the nurse as he draws it up.

Push 0.5.

The nurse does so. The restraints have arrived and we fasten the canvas cuffs around the patient's wrists and ankles and secure them to the bedframe. This act of incarceration feels cruel but I remind myself that it is for her own protection. I lose this tatter of reason as she pushes another rough, wet caw past the pipe in her throat. She produces a rack of hoarse coughs which taper to a slow wheeze and a moan and pulls weakly at the restraints and rolls her head in the semi-stupor of a benzodiazepine haze. Endotracheal tubes are exquisitely unpleasant, which is why intubated patients require sedation. Her eyes are closed, thank god, for I fear the piercing silent plea that might rend me should she crack those heavy hoods.

The bolus of midazolam, another benzodiazepine, on top of whatever else rides unmetabolized through her bloodstream is enough to pull her back under the hypnotic veil and quiet her awful cries. She is finally still save for the slowly effervescing gobs of spittle that leak up from around the tube which lies cradled at the crease of her mouth, bound to her mandible with cloth tape.

We need to get her to the ICU and start a propofol drip before she comes off that midaz, says the Jordanian. Let's pack up.

The residents set to disconnecting lines and piling gear onto the bed between the patient's legs. Someone stomps on a lever to release the brakes and they are off. The wall-mounted telemetry monitor emits a steady whine in their wake, displeased by the absence of signal coming down the wires from its disconnected leads. The floor is littered with medical detritus—empty syringe bodies lie scattered like spent casings among the husks of torn wrappers. A latex glove with black, dried blood on the fingers. Spent and soiled gauze. I reach over to silence the monitor's howl. Now no sound remains but for the demented woman's song. I step into the corridor and leave her to her vigil.

I am exhausted and pale and alone in the hallway. My mind is tangled by the confusion of what I have witnessed. Her seizures looked epileptic at one moment, psychogenic the next—it was impossible to say what was her true affliction. There was no hope of obtaining an encephalogram in the midst of that chaos. Our actions were based on little more than a guess.

If this was an epileptic seizure, we may have saved her life. If it was psychogenic, our treatment was dangerous and traumatic. I remember her agonal cry, muted by the plastic in her throat.

Long strides carry me down the hall and away into the bowels of the hospital. It is silent as a tomb; no patient stirs these wards. IBM wall clocks stud the walls and leer at regular intervals.

I round a corner, and a gloaming sky pours in through a window to pool in front of me. Motes turn like slow spindrift in the light.

I quit the shadows and step into the glow. The sound of my heels against the cool tile beats on ahead of me, like a beacon, down the barren corridor as the dust heels to eddy in my wake.

HOW MUCH REGRET CAN A 6 X 10 ROOM HOLD?

MELODY GREENFIELD

"HAVE YOU EVER HAD A BAD teacher?" I ask Noah. "One that you wanted to fuck?"

"No," he says. "I went to Jewish day school. They were all Israeli. And old."

Old. Like me, I think.

I put him in my mouth and stare up at his too-trusting face. I feel my student relax, then tense up in anticipation. Rhythmically, patiently—I move my hand along the base of him. He is wet with my saliva. Any minute now, he'll release himself to me.

...

Noah is an eighteen-year-old counselor at a sleep-away camp in Ontario's backcountry. I am twelve years his senior. An Angelino who bolted from her live-in boyfriend, from an admissions job that sent her packing, from failures as simple as launching, all to answer phones in a dingy camp office. Here in Canada, I can be anyone. Why not Bad Teacher? Here in Canada, I can be anything. Why not taboo? The irony is not lost on me: coming to get away and choosing someone who'll soon be going away himself, to college. If the circumstances were different, if he were a year younger, I could be going away too, to jail.

The first time, it happens almost innocently. I friend Noah on Facebook. He replies with a smiley face. Fifteen minutes later, he's in my bunk: dirty cot, sandy linoleum floor. Thirty minutes later, he kisses me with a mouth that's thick and soft and full of wild suggestions, like role-play.

The second time, he mounts me, smelling like bug spray and boy, then whispers, "This just isn't working." He has a strange grimace on his face, and it doesn't look like the kind of contorted ugliness a man makes before finishing.

I don't tell him this, but it isn't working for me either, not that morality stands in my way. I've played Bad Teacher before, only then I was twenty-one, and my student was a sixteen-year-old counselor-in-training. Despite Noah's inexperience, it isn't even bad sex. He is gentle and slow, which I don't expect. He has good instincts, too. The problem is the condom. "It's like fucking with your clothes on," I explain before suggesting he take it off.

"I don't think that's a good idea," Noah says nervously, shifting his gaze away from me. It doesn't occur to me that by *that*, he might mean losing his virginity to a woman when he is just a boy. It doesn't occur to me that by that, he might mean playing Bad Teacher or choosing me as his first lover.

I wave his worry away with the flick of my wrist to match the flick of our tongues. "Keep the condom on then. Don't worry. Just relax. You're doing great," I assure him, the way teachers do. For a moment, he loses himself to the rainforest sounds on my Sharper Image noise machine. For a moment, he becomes a snake: astride me, writhing, charmed. *Good job,* I tell him with the low purr of my moan. *Gold star,* I imply with lips parted in mock ecstasy. *Way to go. Pat on the back. Thumbs up.* With my throaty teacher's voice, I give him every encouragement. With the thrust of my hip, I offer him everything but an out, as he reverts back to that scrunched-up face. As he has his first sexual experience and hates it.

...

You should know: There's something about innocence and almond-colored eyes and dark, tousled hair that undoes me. There's something about uncertainty, hesitation, a shaky tongue on my wanting breast that makes me as filthy as the 6 x 10 room bearing witness. There's something about secrecy, flashlights, a furtive knock on a thin wooden door, a bed-side picture of the people I left behind, something about playing a role—Bad Teacher—and seeing it all the way through. There's something about the power in taking someone else's away. Something about doing something illicit and immoral just because you can.

...

With his sweet eyes closed and one hand resting lightly on my head, Noah listens to his teacher. Just breathe and let yourself go, I instruct him as he oozes warm liquid onto my tongue. I gulp hard, swallowing the whole mess, then wipe my mouth with the back of my hand and put an ear to his hairless chest.

I think, Easy clean up.

I think, Brava, teacher.

I think, You've still got it.

Distance tells me: I didn't think at all.

Seasons

Alan Lightman

IN THE FALL OF 1969, THERE were 500,000 American troops in Vietnam. The death of Ho Chi Minh caused only a brief interruption in the fifteen-year-old war. And I, beginning my senior year in college, was faced with the first real challenge to a life of privilege and ease. I was thrown into the national lottery for the draft. It was the first selective service lottery in the United States since 1942. World War II, of course, had been a "popular" war. My father had been constantly afraid of dying on the beaches of Italy or Sicily, but he had not hesitated to enlist when he came of age, nor had any of his friends. My friends, by contrast, did everything possible to escape military service. They were usually successful. Many got educational deferments simply for being in college. Louis, a quiet boy with a brooding intelligence, had dressed up as a Cherokee Indian for his physical examination, including warpaint and feathers, and received a psychiatric release. Others moved to Canada and were sent money from home. But the new lottery seemed a great equalizer of classes and backgrounds. Everyone faced the same odds. Each birth date was to be assigned a number by a toss of the dice. Local draft boards would begin drafting at number 1 and work their way upward.

The drawing was made on December 1 at 8:00 p.m. Eastern Standard Time. Only the day before, on a Sunday, I had returned from Thanksgiving vacation and a grand dinner with my parents and brothers and cousins. After dinner, my mother, determined to be gay, placed a bossa nova album on the record player and made all of us dance with her barefoot in the living room. Now, a few evenings later, I sat anxiously with my roommates in our comfortable Ivy League dormitory room, listening to the radio. The scent of marijuana hung in the air. I imagined millions of other young men, short-order cooks in hamburger joints and gas station attendants trying to close for the night and other students in their rooms, all listening to their radios. Three hundred and sixty-six capsules were plucked from a cylindrical glass bowl in a government room in Washington, DC. The first birthday chosen was September 14. I didn't know anyone born on that day, but I felt sorry for the poor devils. My birth date was chosen 280 draws later. I was never called. About a quarter of my classmates ended up in some kind of military service, that year or later.

Oddly, I remember that fall as intensely beautiful. Autumn had never been a particularly engaging season in Tennessee, where I had grown up, but here, up along the East Coast, the air was so clear and transparent that you felt you might see to the curve of the earth. I recall often hearing an extraordinary concert from a maple tree outside my dormitory window. Hundreds of field finches had decided to roost in that tree for the season. The field finch is a small sparrow-sized bird with a delicate pointed tail. The bird does not twitter or chirp but instead gives out a continuous drawn-out song. When hundreds sing in unison, the sound is an unbroken chorus, with the effect on the hearing like that of a waterfall on the sight, a multitude of tiny droplets combining to make one sweeping flow. The birds stayed until the end of October, then one day were suddenly gone in their migration south.

The lottery disturbed me in many ways. I had lived a life of self-imposed blindness, not just the blindness that comes with financial good fortune and social entitlement. There was, of course, the real possibility of being sent to Vietnam and killed. But this outcome was so unimaginable that it never entered my consciousness. I had stood on the sidelines in naive disbelief as my classmates tried to batter down the front door to the Institute for Defense Analysis. I avoided the bonfires. When a young assistant professor sitting next to me at dinner one night lit a match to his draft card and invited us students to join him, I admired his boldness but didn't have a shred of understanding of what he had done. The lottery forced a vast, unwanted world on me, and the sensation was a painful gush of blood through the veins. Particularly distressing was the element of randomness, the uncertainty. I wanted to make decisions. I would go on to graduate school or I wouldn't. I would pursue a particular young woman or I wouldn't. I would leave my bicycle out in the courtyard at night or I would haul it down to the basement.

Science, for me, had been a source of certainty. I was a physics major, and physics reduced the world to its irreducible particles and forces. It is a banality to say that science holds a reductionist view of the world, and even a twenty-one-year-old knew that life wasn't so simple. But science, especially physics, provides a powerful illusion of simplicity and certainty. Textbooks on physics rarely offer any discussion of the history of the subject, with its wrong turns and prejudices and human passions. Instead, there are Laws. And the Laws seduce with their beauty and precision. Every action has an equal and opposite reaction. The gravitational force between two masses varies inversely with the square of the distance between them. Even Heisenberg's quantum Uncertainty Principle, which proclaimed that the future cannot be determined from the past, gave a definite mathematical formula for containing uncertainties, like a soundproof room built around someone who is screaming. More than its purity and grace, physics was Certainty. And Certainty, for reasons of my own temperament and perhaps also my middle-class upbringing, was my ally. Archimedes and Euclid had stood for Certainty. Lucretius had invoked the atomistic theory of the world in order to free humankind from the vagaries of the gods.

As a senior I was required to do an independent project, a thesis. For some reason that I still cannot fathom, I chose to do an experimental thesis—that is, to build an apparatus for doing an experiment in physics. I had already shown myself completely incompetent in the laboratory. A gadget that I had constructed for my junior-year lab project caught fire because of faulty wiring. The oscilloscope, a standard tool for circuit design, a big metal box covered with knobs for adjusting voltages and currents, baffled me. On the other hand, I was good at theoretical calculations. I loved going from one equation to the next until arriving at the answer, as definite and unassailable as the area of a circle. I loved the cleanliness of pencils and paper. Why I didn't undertake a thesis in theoretical physics I do not know.

Perhaps it was my choice of thesis advisor, Professor Turgot. There was something about Professor Turgot that I found immensely appealing. He was a big bearlike man, fortyish, beginning to bald, stoop-shouldered, whose shirttails always drooped down behind him. He was not at all the absentminded professor. He could fix me and all I was thinking with one eagle glance. When he lectured in the classroom, he addressed the blackboard rather than his students, as if he were having a private conversation with some mythical being living in the world he had created in equations and diagrams. I knew that this lecturing style was deficient, but it conveyed a lifelong fascination with his subject. I wondered whether I could contain my own passion for science, keep it from thinning out and dispersing for twenty more years, when I would reach the age of Professor Turgot.

Professor T was focused, but at the same time he was humble about the limitations of his knowledge. He sometimes confessed his professional blunders, an error in a calculation, a mispositioning of a target in the cyclotron. The rest of our teachers, almost without exception, projected the impression that they had gotten to where they were on a more or less laser-like trajectory. They had a magnificent self-confidence, which I am sure inspired many of their students. But even I, with my devotion to certainty, did not feel comfortable doing research with such a person. I knew that I made mistakes, and a thesis advisor who did so as well might allow me to graduate with my dignity. After class, Professor T, bulkily slumped against the wall and covered with chalk dust, would sometimes talk to me about his wife.

Almost immediately, he began referring to her as Dorothy, so that when I finally met her, at dinner in the Turgots' small house, I felt as if I knew her. None of the other professors ever mentioned their spouses. I asked Professor T to be my thesis advisor. He grinned and said I would be doing an experimental thesis.

The laboratory where I began working was a huge cavern of a place, resembling a warehouse more than anything else. The space was filled with natural light, from skylights thirty feet overhead, as in an artist's studio. There was always an odd smell in the lab—not an unpleasant smell—of oil and dry ice. Canisters filled with liquid nitrogen sat on the concrete floor. When opened, these would emit a wonderful hissing noise as the liquid bubbled and evaporated and escaped in thick opaline clouds. Along three walls, stretching for a hundred feet, were tabletops and workbenches, oscilloscopes, boxes of capacitors and resistors, odd pieces of metal, rubber tubing, Geiger counters, notebooks with radioactive decay rates handwritten in neat columns of figures. There were always a few novels by Proust and Gide sitting casually on a lab table. Professor T's wife, Dorothy, was a scholar in French literature. I like to think that she sometimes visited the lab in the evening, to keep her husband company when he worked there after hours.

In one corner of the lab, a shower faucet protruded inelegantly from the wall, in case someone accidentally came into bodily contact with a radioactive substance and needed to strip down immediately and wash off. The radiation shower I noted with special interest, as I discovered that I had to confront radioactive atoms on a daily basis. My project was to build a device capable of measuring the radioactive disintegration of excited states of neptunium. Neptunium, discovered in 1940, was the first chemical element produced artificially by humankind. Since its atomic number, 93, was just beyond that of uranium, 92, it was named for Neptune, the planet just beyond Uranus. (Plutonium, at atomic number 94, was named after Pluto.) The idea for my thesis, as it evolved in discussions with Professor T, was that the excited neptunium would be created by bombarding a uranium target in the cyclotron. The disintegrating fragments of the neptunium nuclei, in flight through my apparatus, would cause a gas to scintillate, and these scintillations would be detected by several electronic photomultiplier tubes. By carefully measuring the rate at which neptunium nuclei fragmented, we could learn something about the forces struggling and churning within the atom.

As I stumbled along, writing up the specifications of various parts to be made in the machine shop and then respecifying when the parts didn't fit, I was helped by Dave, Professor T's assistant. Dave was indispensable. He thought the undergraduates were "bloody Communists," and he despised the bearded protest marches, but he was devoted to Professor T and his students, and he was the only person who could get the vacuum pump to behave. A vacuum pump, when working properly, starts out with a coarse, grating sound, like the chug of a locomotive, then graduates to a clicking whine, rising in pitch, and ends with a quiet, smooth hum when a good vacuum has been attained. When there is a leak in the system, the pump never progresses beyond the rough, grating chugs. On a number of occasions, I had to pump all the air out of my tangle of brass fittings and Mylar meshes, down to a billionth of an atmosphere. After applying epoxy and Glyptal to all the suspicious joints, we would turn on the vacuum pump. Dave understood that pump, as well as most things in the lab. His understanding went even further than that. I believe he was romantically involved with the woman who delivered small supplies to the lab. After her delivery each week, she would stand at an outside window and look in at him, sadly and longingly. That winter Dave and I were often the only people in the lab, me puzzling over response curves of the photomultiplier tubes and him quietly fixing some gadget that had broken. Occasionally I had to stop and walk over to an electric heater for warmth. Outside, the snow lay across the ground in a vast white silence. Then I would hear a squeaking and crunching, distant at first but gaining in volume, the sound of Professor Turgor's galoshes in the snow as he walked along the path from his office to the lab to check up on his charges.

My apparatus passed all of its preliminary tests, but I never did truly believe that the final experiment would work, and I don't think Professor Turgot did either. When it was time to insert the apparatus into the cyclotron in another building, I received a mysterious message that the cyclotron couldn't be scheduled until a few months after I'd graduated. "I'll write you about the results," Professor T kindly said to me and gave me high marks on my endless drawings of sideviews and topviews and calculations of solid angles and efficiencies. Professor Turgot never wrote and I never asked.

One spring afternoon, soon after Nixon had ordered the invasion of Cambodia, the department of physics had an extraordinary meeting. All the physics faculty and students crowded together into a small room to discuss our departmental response to the student riots taking place on campus. With neatly chalked equations still on the blackboard from some previous hour, faculty members got up one by one and delivered their views on the war. Most were strongly opposed but not all. There were brief and passionate speeches about the nature of democracy, the rights of governments, the purpose of education, moral responsibility. I could hardly recognize these people dressed up like our measured professors. The little room became a struggling upside-down box. I needed air. The discussion turned to a practical matter. What should the department do with its students who were cutting their classes? In the end, the faculty decided to exempt seniors from their final exams and, in some cases, their theses. I reeled out of the room. To my dizzy and confused mind, randomness had finally won out. The world was a jumble of mistaken adventures, crossed wires, mirrors at odd angles. Certainty was a deception. And for me, at that moment in my life, there was either certainty or randomness, nothing in between.

I called Andrew, a roommate from freshman year and a quiet boy like myself. We walked to the lake a mile away and went sailing. It was early May. The breeze was so light that we finally lowered the sails and just drifted, half-asleep in the hot, thick air. We took off our shirts. Soon we were coasting near one of the shores, passing below willow trees that hung down into the boat and tickled our faces with their soft filigree leaves. Finally, a large branch got tangled in the mast and stopped our motion altogether, and we just lay there, enjoying the shade. I got up from my practically prone position and saw that our boat was surrounded by lilies, floating just next to the shore. A few had started to bloom, in luscious white flowers with a speck of purple at their centers. We lay there for hours.

And as we lay there, accidents happened all around us. A bird landed in a nearby tree for no reason and began singing, then flew off just as unexpectedly. Twigs snapped. Clouds changed shape. Grasses rustled with the movements of unseen animals. The earth wobbled imperceptibly on its axis, as bits of cosmic debris randomly bombarded it from space. One such piece of debris, billions of years in the past, had struck with unusual force and cocked the planet over, producing a tilt of twenty-three degrees, producing uneven heating as the earth orbited the sun, producing the seasons. A crumpled piece of paper slowly drifted past in the water, caught on a stick. Some writing on it had become smeared and illegible, perhaps a schedule of someone's appointments, or a note to a lover.

TRANSLATIONS

TRANS

LA

TIONS

OUR MARTYRS

FAROUK GOWEDA

TRANSLATED BY WALID ABDALLAH & ANDY FOGLE

Inside their tombs, our martyrs are whispering,
Oh God we are coming back.

On land they are lifting their hands,
and their voices grow in the silence of the grave:
Oh God we are coming back.

Stones fall, ashes rise, and their eyes beam,
Oh God we are coming back.

Our martyrs stepped out of their coffins,
lined up and raised the shout:
Shame on you cowards.
Our home is sold, our nation
a herd of sheep, and you sleep.

Our martyrs travel to Al Aqsa Mosque,
they pray in the churches of Lebanon,
they wander the streets of Jerusalem,
they break into prisons in every land.

They rise from the ashes of the captive home
and preach on every corner of a beaten nation.

They call in the midst of massacres,
God is greater than this man-made world,

God is greater than this man-made world,
God is greater than this man-made world.

Our martyrs are approaching, their shouts echoing
on the walls of Beirut. They gather in the streets
to fight in darkness despite the pale light.

In homes bound by humiliation and madness, they call,
Oh God we are coming back.
One day our coffins will light all of Jerusalem.

They are coming back to break into the castle.

...

On every corner, they ask the cowards,
Why did you tolerate the wolf, sleeping
amidst sheep, a home as whole as the universe
auctioned off, overrun with rats?

Cowards who sold out our broken home,
our living ancestors, there you are
on the screen, drunk in the fuss,
walking Death, hypocrisy, and control,
we will rid our holy dead of you,
and of the irony of the age.

Oh God we are coming back.

Don't believe that people killed
in a battle for God are dead,
they are still alive in God.

...

Our martyrs, roaring on every corner of the land,
streams of them asking,
Oh living, what are you doing?

Every day you're double-crossed and slain
like sheep, surrendering your rights,
running like rats to the wolves,
leaving your people weeping
while you are prostrate before America's
dollars and the images on screen.

Rats in all sorts of compromising ways.

And in the mad laughter of calamity,
a nation is sold into collapse.

Two images collapse into one:

while kneeling,
your heads under their shoes,
and our Arab Jerusalem,
given to wolves by the drunken.

...

With Lebanon adrift in blood, and tyranny
on the prowl, our martyrs shout
from every corner, *Does honor
have a place? Where have the rebels
disappeared? Why have the sellouts fled?*

The silent, the forgetful, and the two-tongued
all keep their mouths shut.
If you ask, they give you official nonsense.
If you ask, you get a bullet in the eye.

...

When you march in the parade of commerce
you wind up sold. History shows traitors
no mercy. The flood washes
over all of you chasing death
with the ad-man chasing you
to sell you tomorrow in the slave market.

Our priests are oblivious in their seats,
drunk on reign and rule.

Our people in prison-darkness. All of them asleep.

When do the sleeping awaken?
When the sleeping wake.

Untitled

Vladimir Markov

translated by Boris Dralyuk

My life slips from my mind—
days, objects, faces, towns.
All I remember now
are rattling, wailing trains.

Look round, nothing has changed:
I'm in third class once more,
with eggshells on the floor . . .
Seats shine like greasy skin.

Tomorrow is a pond
obscured by scum, while my
whole life lies on my palm,
weblike, in some strange tongue.

1947

LA MEMORIA

JAVIER ETCHEVARREN

TRANSLATED BY JESSE LEE KERCHEVAL

THE MEMORY

My father came home drunk
after several weeks
with no news of him.
He demanded the rent money,
shouting, stinking.

My brothers remember it:
my father tried to hit my mother.
My mother remembers it:
I was two years old and
she sat me high up on the wall.

I don't remember it.

La memoria

Mi padre vino borracho
después de varias semanas
sin noticias de él.
Reclamaba el dinero del alquiler
con gritos fétidos.

Mis hermanos lo recuerdan:
mi padre intentó pegarle a mi madre.
Mi madre lo recuerda:
yo tenía dos años de edad y me sentó sobre un muro.

Yo no lo recuerdo.

EL PARQUE

JAVIER ETCHEVARREN

TRANSLATED BY JESSE LEE KERCHEVAL

THE PARK

Swings.
A sandbox.
Tunnels.
Dozens of trees.
Places where I could hide myself.

The boy ran through the park.

The grass grew.
A garbage dump formed.
By day, drug addicts frequented it.
By night, homeless slept there.

The boy avoided the park.

Chain link fencing, bars.
Construction material and machines.
Children without swings
or sandbox or tunnels or places to hide themselves.

The man writes about the park.

El parque

Hamacas.
Un arenal.
Túneles.
Decenas de árboles.
Lugares donde esconderme.

El niño corría por el parque.

Creció el pasto.
Se formó un basural.
De día lo frecuentaban drogadictos.
De noche dormían indigentes.

El joven evitaba el parque.

Los tejidos, las rejas.
Los materiales, las máquinas.
Muchos niños sin hamacas
ni arenal, ni túneles ni lugares donde esconderse.

El hombre escribe sobre el parque.

FÁBULA DE UN HOMBRE DESCONSOLADO

JAVIER ETCHEVARREN

TRANSLATED BY JESSE LEE KERCHEVAL

FABLE OF AN INCONSOLABLE MAN

A man is made
of little things:
the rubble of a cloud,
a library set on fire,
a cry of love.

Sometimes he abandons himself
in an avenue
on his way through the night.

He illustrates with words
each disaster that announces its name.
He embraces the vertigo
of restless knowledge.
He still has the smile of his childhood
but laughs at his story.

Because every man carries a child
sometimes he neglects it.
One life is not enough
for so many memories.

Because every child carries a man,
past or future.

One body is not enough
for so many fables
without comfort or consolation.

FÁBULA DE UN HOMBRE DESCONSOLADO

Un hombre se hace
con pocas cosas:
los escombros de una nube,
una biblioteca incendiada,
un llanto de amor.

A veces se abandona
en una avenida
en tránsito hacia la noche.

Ilustra con palabras el fracaso
que enuncia su nombre.
Arropa el vértigo
de saberse inquieto.
Mantiene la sonrisa de su infancia
y la risa de su historia.

Porque todo hombre arrastra un niño.
A veces lo descuida.
No basta sólo una vida
para tantas memorias.

Porque todo niño arrastra un hombre
pasado o futuro.
No basta sólo un cuerpo
para tantas fábulas
sin consuelo.

UNTITLED

IVAN ELAGIN

TRANSLATED BY BORIS DRALYUK

My neighbors hang on walls facing my flat,
in heavy frames, behind thick glass:
a woman dressed in plaid sits deep in thought,
a student stoops above his writing desk.
While farther off, two girls, bored and alone,
have pressed their foreheads up against their panes.
A year will pass, I'll stare out at the same
old page in this, my album made of stone.

Kule na wodzie

Krystyna Dąbrowska

translated by Mira Rosenthal

Water Walking Balls

When I think of us, I recall
the latest trendy pastime at the beach:
people enclosed in huge blow-up balls
trying to walk on water.

So it was with us—each in our own bubble,
not laughing but rather ashamed and unable
to step toward each other without stumbling
or to hide how the slightest gesture is a struggle.

Tottering, knocking against walls,
we pretended to be acrobats.
One against the other played captain
of a self-sufficient ship.

We could have tried to burst the plastic,
even with a desperate, clumsy slip.
But what if it worked? This, after all,
we feared far more than failure.

Thinking of us, I see people over there:
the bubbles that held them had strings
to pull them ashore if they ran out
of air or grew tired of the game.

KULE NA WODZIE

Gdy o nas myślę, przypominam sobie
zabawę modną ostatnio nad morzem:
ludzie zamknięci w nadmuchanych kulach
próbują chodzić po wodzie.

Tak było z nami – każde w swojej bańce,
lecz zamiast śmiechu wstyd, że nie umiemy
zrobić ku sobie kroku bez potknięcia,
ukryć, że najdrobniejszy gest to walka.

Chwiejąc się, obijając o ściany,
udawaliśmy parę akrobatów,
jedno przed drugim grało kapitana
samowystarczalnego statku.

Mogliśmy starać się rozerwać plastik
choćby desperackim, niezdarnym ruchem,
lecz gdyby się udało? Tego przecież
bardziej się baliśmy niż porażki.

Myśląc o nas, widzę tamtych ludzi:
bańki, w których byli, miały sznurki,
by ściągnąć je na brzeg, jeśli zabraknie
powietrza albo zabawa się znudzi.

REVIEWS

REVIEWS

ARE THEY REALLY SERIOUS?
KOERTGE, DUHAMEL, & WEBB
WILLIAM TROWBRIDGE

VAMPIRE PLANET: NEW & SELECTED POEMS, RON KOERTGE; RED HEN PRESS, 2016
ISBN: 978-1-59709-760-4; $17.95; 144 PP.

BLOWOUT, DENISE DUHAMEL; UNIVERSITY OF PITTSBURGH PRESS, 2013
ISBN: 978-0-8229-6236-6; $15.95; 92 PP.

BRAIN CAMP, CHARLES HARPER WEBB; UNIVERSITY OF PITTSBURGH PRESS, 2015
ISBN: 978-0-8229-6338-7; $15.95; 102 PP.

IN THEIR 2010 ANTHOLOGY *SERIOUSLY FUNNY*, Barbara Hamby and David Kirby note what many readers have thought, that "much of American poetry lacks humor." That lack might have its roots as far back as Aristotle's comment in *The Poetics*: "Comedy is, as we have said, an imitation of characters of a lower type—not however in the full sense of the word 'bad,' the ludicrous being merely a subdivision of the ugly." Humor, then, is the base material that must be refined out of works intended to register high on the literary-o-meter, where tragedy dwells. Poetry is conventionally put up there too—as a higher form of expression than that prosaic stuff, prose. To many, I'm afraid, it follows that poetry should be very lean on humor, and great poetry should be downright humorless. Such purity has seemed much less imperative to our prose writers. Robert Penn Warren, in his essay "Pure and Impure Poetry," defines "pure poetry," of which he disapproves, as "that which excludes ugly words and ugly phrases—all things which call us back to the world of prose and imperfection." Surely humor, great deflater of the highfalutin, belongs in Warren's list of impurities. In good, "impure" poetry, as Auden said the Old Masters showed us, ". . . even the dreadful martyrdom must run its course / Anyhow in . . . some untidy spot / Where . . . the torturer's horse scratches its innocent behind on a tree."

Flannery O'Connor has said, ". . . all comic novels that are any good must be about matters of life and death." Some of our best contemporary poets, as well as prose writers, also see comedy and seriousness as inseparable. Of course, I'm not talking of "light verse," if the term refers to poetry written merely to amuse—though there's sometimes a very hazy border between the light and the seriously funny. And I'm not talking about poets who write the occasional seriocomic poem. Rather, I mean poets for whom comedy is essential to their view of the human condition.

The humor gap between prose and poetry seems to have gotten slimmer even before *Seriously Funny*. I think that's at least partially due to Charles Harper Webb's pioneering anthology, derived from his 1987 essay "Five Stand Up Poets." That anthology was titled *Stand Up Poetry: The Poetry of Los Angeles and Beyond* and then, in a 2002 revision, retitled, *Stand Up Poetry: An Expanded Anthology*. Defining the term, Webb says, "Not every Stand Up poem is fall-down funny, but many make skillful use of humor. Playful, irreverent, and high-spirited, these poems employ the techniques of comedy: timing, absurdity, hyperbole." The change in the after-colon part of the anthology title implies that, in the intervening years, such poetry has spread well beyond the West Coast. As Webb notes, it may be that "mainstream poetry has absorbed Stand Up in the way that a large tribe absorbs a smaller one." Still holding back this trend is the abiding elevation of the purely serious over the seriously funny. And our culture may never shake that bias completely, especially when it comes to poetry.

Among the growing number of seriocomic poets are famous ones, like Collins, Goldbarth, and Hoagland. I want to discuss the latest books of three other seriously funny poets who have, as yet, received less recognition.

...

The first of these is Ron Koertge's *Vampire Planet*. In this new-and-selected collection, Koertge continues writing in his witty, conversational style about middle-class life, popular culture, and fairy tales. A Koertge poem is like a chat over a beer with a pal who's a sly, gifted storyteller. But its chattiness isn't shallow or, as he as he quips in one poem, "loquacious." His poems are lean and well-crafted, with ample gravitas not far beneath the surface. The fact that they are easy, even fun to read, should never be taken as a lack of sophistication or of literary merit—despite the present trend toward "difficult" or "oblique" poetry. Raised in a home where "similes usually meant a trip to the bathroom where my mouth was washed out with Ivory soap," Koertge is nevertheless a master of fresh and on-target tropes. A young girl's date is "he who rose from the sludge of other boys to stand out like / red oxide." In a visit to his grandmother's house, "A mirror / looked back at me, glad to have something / new to think about." His mother's empty threats to discipline him as a child are "The butter knife of Damocles." He watches a good poem by an elementary school student sail away from the poet "like a corsage pinned to the lapel of the sky." At the end of a poem about the Hardy Boys, the boys finally ask themselves, "Are these beautiful / hometown girls shadowy doors leading to the mysteries / no amount of sleuthing can ever solve?" There are moments in Koertge's poems that raise the proverbial hairs on your neck. In "When We Finish the Workshop," the speaker accompanies an elderly woman, who's impatient with how long it takes to get a poem in a magazine, as she hands out copies of hers to everyone she runs into at a farmer's market.

> For a moment as dusk struggles not to give way
> to night everyone seems to be reading, everyone
> except the lady who sharpens knives.
>
> She does not lift the gleaming blade from
> the grinding wheel, perhaps because the dark
> figure waiting has told her he is in a hurry.

...

Denise Duhamel's collection *Blowout* illustrates one of the most important elements of comedy: pain. Mark Twain said, "The secret source of Humor is not in joy but sorrow. There is no humor in heaven." Duhamel's book catalogues a series of sorrows that came close together in her life: divorce, near bankruptcy, ill health, death of a parent. What keeps these poems, most in first-person, from seeming a whine-laden stream of self-pity is her use of brilliant, self-deprecating humor, reminiscent of Woody Allen's best stand-up routines. Who can resist a poem titled "Self-Portrait in Hydrogen Peroxide" or "My Strip Club" or "Cleopatra Invented the First Vibrator." She parodies her worry-wart tendency in "Worst Case Scenario."

> There's blood in your stool. Your car stalls at a light. Your mannerisms become stilted. You stand still. You become stale. You fall off your stilts. He [ex-husband] slits his wrists. You make a fist. You get up too fast. You miss the feast. He foists himself on someone else. You end up in a state-run nursing home. You never grow up. Your hunger makes you queasy. You abandon your quest. They call you Quasimodo.

Through most of the collection, the speaker finds that love is pretty much what she found in fourth grade with a fat kid who said he wanted to be her boyfriend.

—it was fall

and that's when my asthma flared up. One time my nose started to bleed
and, because I didn't have any tissues, the fat boy gave me
his science worksheet, then a big maple leaf, to catch the blood.
So what if he couldn't dance? That was love.

Sometimes humor is the only defense against despair, and Duhamel uses it brilliantly, turning from it only toward the end of the collection, where she finally does seem to find romantic love.

...

Charles Harper Webb has not only called attention early to seriocomic poets, he is one of the best. His style is more formal than Koertge's or Duhamel's. Though he writes in free verse, most of his poems are in stanzas, and the iamb's shadow moves behind his lines. *Brain Camp* is perhaps his best book so far—a dazzling collection reflecting Webb's interest and erudition in music, physical science, and psychology. His wit and verbal dexterity can be seen in "Hospital."

Hot spittle sizzling on pain's grill.
Hopcycle: a gamboling bike. Hopsickle:
bouncy tooth-chilling, bad for you.

Opposite of hope's fiddle. No
"Soldier's Joy." No "Jolie Blonde."
Losspital: place where losers

meet. Hospice: little. (How big
do death rooms have to be?)
Hiss bottle, has pickle. Ass brittle—

Like Koertge and Duhamel, Webb swims against the icy current of postmodernism, which he describes in "Postmodernism Missed the Opry" as

. . . a city boy who's never been
so lonesome he could cry—who'd never

walk the line, sigh, "Hello, walls," or waltz
across Texas—who thinks he's too smart

to place a rose from her own garden on the grave
of his wife of fifty years—who hides,
in an ice chest that should be full of longnecks,
his really and truly cold, cold heart.

Webb's heart is large and warm, and in a book that's a treasury of imaginative leaps, he demonstrates that again and again. In "Moth," at death, the soul, as gray moth, "flies out the least obvious ear— // not to heaven" but to a leaf in the nearest tree and "seeps inside it."

That is why children rake leaves into mountains

to slide down, and why men fire up
a pile of leaves on a cold day and stare

into the blaze, and will say only, "I like
the smell." "I like the heat." "I like the light."

All three of these poets celebrate the glories, pains, and pratfalls of being human—sometimes wryly, sometimes hilariously, always focused on matters of life and death. Their reader-friendly poems should help contemporary poetry matter to those new to it and matter once again to those spurned by postmodernism's cold, cold heart.

THIS SHOULD BE WRITTEN IN THE PRESENT TENSE

FICTION BY HELLE HELLE, TRANSLATED FROM THE DANISH BY MARTIN AITKEN

SOFT SKULL PRESS, 2016; ISBN: 978-1-593766-337; $15.95; 208 PP.

REVIEWED BY PEDRO PONCE

IN THE DEFT AND SUBTLY ENGROSSING *This Should Be Written in the Present Tense*, Helle Helle's first novel to be published in English, the Danish author pulls off a balancing act far more difficult than Dorte, the story's unassuming narrator, might admit. While claiming to be a student in Copenhagen, Dorte instead spends much of her time wandering—in the city where she supposedly studies, around her rented home, or through memories of her ex-boyfriend Per. The short chapters give her story the tentative quality of a life in progress:

> It was Saturday morning, I felt like I ought to be doing something. Finishing the unpacking and taking the empty boxes out into the shed, for instance, or having a bath. Fresh air would do me good as well, I could at least go over the road and walk down the little path by the flats to the supermarket, buy some vegetables and some apples for the train that coming week.

Dorte's ruminations are interrupted when she realizes that her new place comes with an apple tree; the unsettled awkwardness of arrival is briefly broken by a sense of familiarity and ownership. The novel alternates between past and present, but neither is idealized. Per is only a temporary distraction from the restlessness that permeates Dorte's character, and eventually leads her to cheat with Per's cousin. Alone in the present, Dorte searches for direction in her day-to-day life and writerly aspirations. Her guide through the flux is her divorced aunt Dorte—the protagonist's namesake—who provides a touchstone for the novel's nomadic atmosphere: "The times I lived with her she always had a laugh sticking a note up next to her name on the door so it said *Dorte Hansen x 2*" (author's italics). What ultimately holds the book together is Dorte's voice, a supple, mature instrument that shades happenstance with retrospective clarity. By turns halting and adept, banal and poetic, *This Should Be Written in the Present Tense* offers discoveries in its digressions, in prose that appears effortless.

THE SLEEP GARDEN

FICTION BY JIM KRUSOE

TIN HOUSE BOOKS, 2016; ISBN: 978-1-94104-018-8; $15.95; 342 PP.

REVIEWED BY ANN BEMAN

JIM KRUSOE HAS WRITTEN HIS SIXTH novel as metafictional stage play, with his stage a sub-terranean apartment building invoking a mashup of *Friends*-like sitcoms, *Big Brother*-esque reality shows, and *Waiting for Godot*–ish theater of the absurd. The five main characters live in a dreamlike stasis, frustrated by lofty ambitions, yet never able to break from their routines. Known as "the Burrow" (hello, Kafka), the claustrophobic dwelling is riddled with mirrors: "So everything reflects everything else, like living in a fun house . . . [and] while it's true, they do reflect the light, they also multiply the dark." Interwoven with the Burrow-dwellers' stories are those of a retired sea captain, a sociopathic former child actor, and a pair of behind-the-scenes technicians who monitor/maintain the Burrow and serve as its Greek chorus.

...

Thus the novel navigates a labyrinth of pastiches, blending theatrical styles as well as writing styles, from prose to letters to comparison charts to screenplays. One character aspires to write a sitcom called—what else?—"The Burrow," because stories are "the addiction that keeps the poor old nag of the human race running around the track." For those of us nags who pick up the pace when it comes to humor and surreality, *The Sleep Garden* is a solid bet.

She Came From Beyond!

Fiction by Nadine Darling

THE OVERLOOK PRESS, 2015; ISBN: 978-1-46831-152-5; $26.95; 272 PP.

REVIEWED BY SIEL JU

IN THESE DAYS OF INTERNET CELEBRITIES and reality TV stars-turned-politicians, Nadine Darling's sly satire seems not so far from reality. *She Came From Beyond!* tells the story of one Easy Hardwick, an easy-on-the-eyes twenty-something who finds microfame among geeks by cavorting around in strange costumes on a cable access sci-fi parody show. Small stardom isn't the main complication in Easy's uneasy life, however. The real trouble is her family—a family that suddenly mushrooms in size when Easy becomes pregnant with twins after falling into bed with a charming guy called Harrison—who neglected to mention his wife and two kids. The bizarre complications of Easy's life at times get tiringly overwrought, since on top of all the Harrison shenanigans, Easy also has two gay dads with their own multiple subplots, including, but not limited to, celebrity decoys, eating disorders, and sexual confusion. Still, there's much to admire in Darling's entertaining spectacle, like Easy's wry sense of humor. Pointing out that the cable show opened a lot of doors for her, Easy adds these were "Sad, pointless doors that led nowhere, like a display of doors at a place that sells doors." Despite the many setbacks that assail her, Easy remains spunky and hopeful and engaged—revealing how human connection persists even amidst pop culture obsessions, chat room subcultures, and life's inevitable, insistent twists and turns.

SERGIO Y.

FICTION BY ALEXANDRE VIDAL PORTO, TRANSLATED BY ALEX LADD

EUROPA EDITIONS, 2016; ISBN: 978-1-60945-327-5; $16.00; 160 PP.

REVIEWED BY DANNY CAINE

SERGIO Y. TRACES THE RELATIONSHIP BETWEEN a renowned psychiatrist in São Paolo, Brazil, and a troubled young client. After a too-brief series of sessions, the client (Sergio) moves to New York and disappears from the life of his therapist, the book's narrator Armando. Only gradually does Armando discover how much he didn't know about Sergio, who had moved to New York to live as a woman named Sandra. Armando's efforts to unpack the mystery send him on a journey of transatlantic soul-searching, wondering "What role might I have had in the tragic fate of Sergio Y? Was I as important as I deemed myself to be when I heard he was happy?"

...

This is the first appearance in English translation for Porto, a Harvard-educated diplomat and lawyer. Alex Ladd's clear and simple translating lends poise to Porto's multifaceted story. After reading *Sergio Y.*'s sensitive treatment of transgender identity, it should come as no surprise that Porto also works as a human rights activist; in one stirring passage, Sergio's mother explains, "He was looking for a way to be happy . . . Yes, after he became Sandra, Sergio was happy . . . as a woman, he found happiness." The novel deftly explores Sergio's search for happiness via his transformation into Sandra from many angles, including the broadly historical and the achingly intimate, as it questions just how much responsibility a therapist has over an identity in crisis. In an era where efforts to strip transgender people of their dignity are common headline news, *Sergio Y.* reads like a much-needed tonic.

GATEWAY TO PARADISE: STORIES

FICTION BY MATTHEW VOLLMER

PERSEA BOOKS, 2015; ISBN: 978-0-89255-466-9; $15.95; 184 PP.

REVIEWED BY SIEL JU

WHY DO GOOD PEOPLE MAKE BAD choices? This question is at the center of Matthew Vollmer's short stories, which often feature likeable men making dopey mistakes. In "Probation," a bored father aims a laser pointer at a police helicopter—then breaks his resulting house arrest to look for his missing daughter. In "Scoring," a hapless husband gets pulled in by the unexpected come-ons of a beauty counter clerk—who turns out to use sexual entrapment to save souls for Christ. In "The Visiting Writer," a discontented professor meets a fascinating famous author—and embarrassingly misreads her simple requests. Even the stories that feature female protagonists center around male shortcomings. A sexually withholding husband causes his wife to contemplate a closer relationship with her affectionate pet in "Dog Lover." And in the titular story, a young girl is forced to make some tough choices after her impetuous boyfriend goads her into committing a robbery that goes terribly wrong. Why was she with him in the first place? "It was nice to imagine that she'd found someone good," Vollmer writes. Despite the men's serious shortcomings, these stories are full of humor and insight about the greed, entitlement, self-serving rationalizations, and other human weaknesses common to us all.

CONTRIBUTOR NOTES

WALID ABDALLAH is an Egyptian writer and a lecturer in English language and literature. His books include *Male Domination and Female Emancipation* and *Escape to the Realm of Imagination*, and a collection of short poems called *I Will Always Be There for You*.

HEATHER ALTFELD's first book, *The Disappearing Theatre* won the Poets at Work Book Prize, selected by Stephen Dunn. Her poems appear in *Narrative Magazine, Pleiades, ZYZZY-VA, Poetry Northwest*, and others. She won the 2015 Pablo Neruda Prize for Poetry with Nimrod International Magazine of Poetry and Prose. She lives in Northern California and teaches in the English Department and the Honors Program at California State University, Chico and is a member of the Community of Writers at Squaw Valley.

ANN BEMAN has been writing a book about thumbs forever. *LAR*'s nonfiction editor lives in California's Sierra Nevada with her husband, two whatchamaterriers and a chihuahua in Kernville, on the Kern River, in Kern County (cue the banjoes).

COURTNEY BIRD has an MFA from the University of Montana. Prior to heading west, she attended Princeton University and worked in New York City. Her work has appeared in the *Masters Review*, the *Fairy Tale Review*, and the *Portland Review*. She lives in Seattle, Washington.

POPE BROCK is a writer, teacher and DJ living in Arlington, Massachusetts. He is the author of three books: *Indiana Gothic* (Doubleday/Nan A. Talese), about the murder of his great-grandfather; *Charlatan: America's Most Dangerous Huckster, the Man Who Pursued Him, and the Age of Flimflam* (Crown), about the most successful quack in American history, and *Another Fine Mess: Life on Tomorrow's Moon* (Red Hen Press, forthcoming), a work of what might be called speculative nonfiction. His articles have appeared in *GQ, Esquire, Rolling Stone, London Sunday Times Magazine*, and many other publications. Since 2005 he has taught in the low-residency MFA Writing Program at the University of Nebraska.

REBECCA BROWN is a poet from Chicago, IL. She is a VONA/Voices of our Nations Arts alumna. rebecca has been a teaching artist and dialogue facilitator for eleven years. She is currently crafting her first chapbook collection.

CHRISTOPHER BUCKLEY's *Star Journal: Selected Poems* is published by the Univ. of Pittsburgh Press, fall 2016. His twentieth book of poetry, *Back Room at the Philosophers' Club*, was the winner of the 2015 Lascaux Prize in Poetry. Among several critical collections and anthologies he has edited: *A Condition of the Spitit: The Life and Work of Larry Levis*, 2004, with Alexander Long; *Bear Flag Republic: Prose Poems and Poetics from California*, 2008, and *One for the Money: The Sentence as a Poetic Form*, from Lynx House Press, 2012, both with Gary Young. He has also edited *On the Poetry of Philip Levine: Stranger to Nothing*, Univ. of Michigan Press, 1991, *First Light: A Festschrift for Philip Levine on his 85th Birthday*, 2013, and *Messenger to the Stars: a Luis Omar Salinas New Selected Poems & Reader* for Tebot Bach's Ash Tree Poetry Series.

DANNY CAINE's poems have appeared in *Hobart, Mid-American Review, Midwestern Gothic, New Ohio Review*, and other places. He is author of the *Dispatches from the Factory of Sadness* sports poetry column for *Atticus Review's* "More than Sports Talk". He hails from Cleveland and lives in Lawrence, Kansas where he works at the Raven Bookstore and co-edits *Beecher's Magazine*.

KEVIN CRAFT is the author of *Solar Prominence*, selected by Vern Rutsala for the Gorsline Prize (Cloudbank Books, 2005). He lives in Seattle, and directs the Written Arts Program at Everett Community College. He also directs a summer creative writing program at the University of Washington Rome Center. From 2009–2016 he was the editor of *Poetry Northwest*, and now serves as executive editor of Poetry NW Editions.

KRYSTYNA DĄBROWSKA is a translator, essayist, and author of three books of poetry. Her second collection, *White Chairs* (2012), won the prestigious Kościelski Prize and the inaugural Wisława Szymborska Award. Her poems have been translated into numerous languages and appear regularly in literary magazines in Poland and abroad, including *Akzente, Sinn und Form*, and *Harper's Magazine*. Her translations include the poetry of William Carlos Williams, W. B. Yeats, Thomas Hardy, Thom Gunn and Charles Simic, as well as two early satires of Jonathan Swift. A graduate of the Graphics Department of the Academy of Fine Arts, she lives and works in Warsaw.

Raised in Texas, CLAYTON DALTON studied American history first, medicine second. He is currently a resident in emergency medicine in Boston, MA.

KELLY DAVIO is the poetry editor of *Tahoma Literary Review* and the author of the poetry collections *Burn This House* (Red Hen, 2013) and the forthcoming *The Book of the Unreal Woman* (Salmon) as well as the forthcoming essay collection *It's Just Nerves* (Squares and Rebels). Formerly the Senior Editor of Eyewear Publishing in London, she recently returned to the United States to live and write in the greater New York area.

LAURIE ANN DOYLE is the author of *World Gone Missing*, a book of short stories that includes "Just Ask for Hateman" (appearing here for the first time) and will be released by Regal House Press in 2017. Her work has been published widely in journals and anthologies including *Jabberwock Review, Dogwood Journal, Road Story*, and *Timber*. She teaches writing at the San Francisco Writers Grotto and UC Berkeley. www.laurieanndoyle.com

ROSA DEL DUCA grew up in Montana but now lives in California. Her work has appeared in *CutBank, Grain, River Teeth, CALYX*, and *Mission at Tenth*. When she's not writing, she's cranking out the news at NBC Bay Area, or singing with her folk pop band Hunters, which recently released *We All Go Up the Mountain Alone Together*.

BORIS DRALYUK has translated a number of volumes from Russian and Polish, including, most recently, Isaac Babel's *Red Cavalry* (Pushkin Press, 2014) and *Odessa Stories* (Pushkin Press, 2016). He is the co-editor, with Robert Chandler and Irina Mashinski, of *The Penguin Book of Russian Poetry* (2015) and the editor of *1917: Stories and Poems from the Russian Revolution* (Pushkin Press, 2016).

IVAN ELAGIN (né Matveyev, 1918–1987) was a Russian poet who immigrated to the United States after fleeing the Soviet Union during the Second World War with his first wife, the poet Olga Anstey; they divorced in New York in 1950. Elagin taught Russian literature at the University of Pittsburgh from 1970 until the time of his death.

JAVIER ETCHEVARREN is an Uruguayan poet and the author of the poetry books *Desidia* (Yaugarú, 2009) and *Fábula de un hombre desconsolado* (Yaugarú, 2014). His poems appear in *América invertida: An Anthology of Emerging Uruguayan Poets* (University of New Mexico Press) and have been published in *Drunken Boat, The American Literary Review* and *The Colorado Review*.

ANDY FOGLE has five chapbooks, and poems, translations, memoir, interviews, criticism, and educational research in *South Dakota Review, Teachers & Writers Collaborative, Gargoyle,* and elsewhere. He has been an educator for nineteen years.

BARBARA FRIED's short stories have appeared, among other places, in *Bellevue Literary Review, Subtropics, Guernica,* and *Word Riot.* Her story "The Half-Life of Nat Glickstein" was chosen as a Distinguished Story of 2013 by the editors of Best American Short Stories. Her story "It Goes Without Saying" was a finalist in *Bellevue Literary Review*'s 2013 Fiction Contest. Other of her stories have received recognition in *Glimmer Train, Fish* and *New Millennium* fiction contests. In her day job, she is a law professor at Stanford University, in which capacity she has written widely on political and moral theory for academic and general audiences.

AMY GERSTLER is a writer of poetry, nonfiction, and journalism who lives in Los Angeles. Her eleven poetry collections include *Bitter Angel,* winner of the National Book Critics Circle Award, *Dearest Creature,* a finalist for the *Los Angeles Times* Book Prize, and *Scattered at Sea,* longlisted for the National Book Award.

COREY GINSBERG's work has most recently appeared in such publications as *Hippocampus, Redux, Third Coast, the cream city review,* and *The MacGuffin.* Corey lives in Miami and works as a freelance writer.

FAROUK GOWEDA is an Egyptian poet who has been widely influential in the Arab world. He has published forty-three books, including eighteen collections of poetry and three plays, his work has been translated into several languages, and he has been awarded several national and international prizes.

MELODY GREENFIELD has an MFA in Creative Nonfiction Writing from Antioch University Los Angeles. This LA-native and Pilates instructor has been published in *Brevity, Lunch Ticket,* and *Annotation Nation* and enjoys reading, furthering her Pilates practice, and watching bad TV with her Canadian husband. She uses a pseudonym because of her English-teaching past.

PAUL GUEST is the author of three poetry collections and a memoir. His poems appear in *New England Review, North American Review, Poetry Northwest,* and elsewhere. A Guggenheim Fellow and Whiting Award winner, he teaches in the Creative Writing program at the University of Virginia.

CARMELLA DE LOS ANGELES GUIOL is the 2016 recipient of *Crab Orchard Review*'s Charles Johnson Award for fiction. Her writing has appeared in *The Washington Post, Nustle, The Toast, Thought Catalog, The Normal School, Slag Glass City, Kudzu House, Tahoma Literary Review, The Manifest-Station, Chicken Soup for the Soul*, and elsewhere. You can often find her working in the garden or frolicking in a body of water, but you can always find her writing at www.therestlesswriter.com.

LEE GULYAS and BRENDA MILLER work and write together in Bellingham, WA, where they both teach at Western Washington University. Lee's work has appeared in many journals, such as *Tinerbox, Literary Mama, Sweet, Full Grown People*, and *ReDivider*. Lee is a world traveler who always knows the answer to any question that may arise in casual conversation, because her curiosity is insatiable. Brenda has published five collections of essays, the latest of which is *An Earlier Life* (Overbird Books, 2016). She also co-authored *Tell it Slant*, and *The Pen and the Bell: Mindful Writing in a Busy World*. Brenda fosters dogs, even though it makes her own dog, Abbe, a little jealous. She is a dream to work with.

ROCHELLE HURT is the author of two poetry collections: *In Which I Play the Runaway* (2016), winner of the Barrow Street Book Prize, and *The Rusted City* (White Pine, 2014). She's received awards from *Crab Orchard Review, Arts & Letters, Hunger Mountain, Phoebe, Poetry International*, and the Dorothy Sargent Rosenberg Fund.

MELANIE JEFFREY is a mother, writer, and teacher. She currently teaches English Composition, Creative Writing, and Speech at Cerro Coso Community College in Ridgecrest, California. She finds beauty in the Mojave Desert during her daily commute: Joshua trees, Red Rock Canyon, and poppies.

TROY JOLLIMORE's most recent collection of poetry, *Syllabus of Errors*, was chosen by the *New York Times* as one of the best poetry books of 2015. His previous poetry books are *At Lake Scugog* (2011) and *Tom Thomson in Purgatory*, which won the National Book Critics Circle Award in poetry for 2006. He is also the author of two philosophical works, *Love's Vision* and *On Loyalty*, and has received fellowships from the Bread Loaf Writers Conference, the Stanford Humanities Center, and the Guggenheim Foundation.

SIEL JU's novel-in-stories, *Cake Time*, is the winner of the 2015 Red Hen Press Fiction Manuscript Award and was published in Spring 2017. Siel is also the author of two poetry chapbooks and the recipient of residencies from The Anderson Center and Vermont Studio Center. Her stories and poems appear in *ZYZZYVA*, *The Missouri Review* (Poem of the Week), *The Los Angeles Review*, *Denver Quarterly*, and other places. More of her work can be found at sielju.com.

MEHDI M. KASHANI lives and writes in Toronto, Canada. One of his short stories in Persian won first place in the Sadeq Hedayat 12th Annual Short Story Contest in 2014. His fiction has appeared in *Hobart* and *Litro* and is forthcoming in *The Malahat Review* and *Portland Review*.

MYRON KAUFMAN was born in Brooklyn, NY, in 1927. At the age of sixteen, he joined the Navy, and upon returning from a two-year stint, earned his high school diploma and college degree, and began working as an electrical engineer. Sketching and painting has long been a hobby for Kaufman—his visual art appeared regularly in the Offramp Gallery in Pasadena, CA. In the past several years, his artistic interests have recently turned to writing, and his work has since been published in *BOMB Magazine*.

JESSE LEE KERCHEVAL is the author of the poetry collections *Cinema Muto*, *Dog Angel* and the bilingual poetry collection *Extranjera/ Stranger*. Her translations include *Invisible Bridge/ El puente invisible: Selected Poems of Circe Maia*. She is also the editor of *América invertida: An Anthology of Emerging Uruguayan Poets*.

ARAM KIM is a short story writer. Her works have appeared in *Diagram*, *No Tokens Journal*, *Cosmonauts Avenue*, and elsewhere. She splits her time between Seoul and Santa Clara, CA.

PETER LABERGE is the author of the chapbooks *Makeshift Cathedral* (YesYes Books, 2017) and *Hook* (Sibling Rivalry Press, 2015). His work appears in *Beloit Poetry Journal*, *Best New Poets*, *Harvard Review*, *Iowa Review*, *Pleiades*, *Tin House*, and elsewhere. He is the recipient of a fellowship from the Bucknell University Stadler Center for Poetry and the founder and editor-in-chief of *The Adroit Journal*. He lives in Philadelphia, where he is an undergraduate student at the University of Pennsylvania.

ALAN LIGHTMAN, physicist, essayist, and novelist, is Professor of the Practice of the Humanities at MIT, where he was the first person to receive a joint appointment in the sciences and the humanities. Lightman's writing has appeared in *Harper's, Salon, The New Yorker, The Atlantic*, and many other publications. His widely known *Einstein's Dreams* was an international bestseller, and his novel *The Diagnosis* was a finalist for the National Book Award in fiction. His recent book *The Accidental Universe* was chosen by *Brain Pickings* as one of the best ten books of the year. In spring 2017, Red Hen Press released a new illustrated edition of Lightman's verse narrative *Song of Two Worlds*.

KELLY MAGEE's books include *Body Language*, winner of the Katherine Anne Porter Prize, *The Neighborhood*, from Gold Wake Press, and several collaborative works. Her work has appeared in *Gulf Coast, Crazyhorse, Kenyon Review, Barrelhouse, Booth*, and others. She teaches at Western Washington University. Find her at kellyelizabethmagee.com.

VLADIMIR MARKOV (1920–2013) was one of the world's leading authorities on Russian modernist poetry, especially that of the Russian Futurists. He was also a gifted poet. Markov was born in Petrograd, lost his parents to Stalin's repressions, and ended up in the West after being captured by German troops at the front during the Second World War. He immigrated to the United States in 1949, taught Russian literature at UCLA from 1957 until 1990, and remained in Brentwood until his death in 2013.

JENNIFER MARITZA MCCAULEY is a PhD candidate in creative writing at the University of Missouri. She is presently Contest Editor at *The Missouri Review*, and an associate editor at *Origins Literary Journal*. Her most recent work appears in *Puerto del Sol, Feminist Wire* and *New Delta Review*, among other outlets.

KIMBERLY MEYER is the author of *The Book of Wanderings*. Her other work has appeared in *The Best American Travel Writing, Ploughshares, The Kenyon Review, The Georgia Review, Oxford American, This American Life* and *Texas Monthly*. She teaches in a Great Books program at the University of Houston's Honors College.

MIGUEL MURPHY is the author of *Detainee* and *A Book Called Rats*, winner of the Blue Lynx Prize for poetry. He lives in Southern California where he teaches at Santa Monica College.

JOSEPH OSMUNDSON is a scientist and writer from the rural Pacific Northwest. His writing has appeared or is forthcoming in *The Los Angeles Review of Books, The Kenyon Review, Gawker, The Rumpus, LitHub, The Lambda Literary Review*, and *The Feminist Wire*, where he is an Associate Editor. He's currently a postdoctoral fellow in systems biology at NYU. Find him at www.josephosmundson.com and on Twitter @reluctantlyjoe.

PEDRO PONCE is the author of *Dreamland*, a novel forthcoming from Satellite Press.

ELLEN RACHLIN is the author of *Permeable Divide* (forthcoming 2017), *Until Crazy Catches Me* and two chapbooks, *Waiting for Here* and *Captive to Residue*. Her poems have appeared in various journals and anthologies including *American Poetry Review*, *Granta*, *Literary Imagination*, *Confrontation*, and *Court Green*. She received her MA from Antioch. She serves as Treasurer of the Poetry Society of America and works in finance.

MIRA ROSENTHAL is the author of *The Local World* and translator of two books by Polish poet Tomasz Różycki. Her work has received numerous awards, including an NEA Fellowship, a Stegner Fellowship, a PEN/Heim Translation Grant, and the Northern California Book Award. She is Assistant Professor of Poetry Writing at Cal Poly.

RHIAN SASSEEN's work has appeared in *Aeon*, *Pacific Standard*, *The Awl*, and others. More can be found at her website, rhiansasseen.com.

MARTHA SILANO's most recent books include an expanded second edition of *What the Truth Tastes Like* (Two Sylvias Press 2015), *Reckless Lovely* (Saturnalia Books 2014); and, with Kelli Russell Agodon, *The Daily Poet: Day-By-Day Prompts For Your Writing Practice*. She edits *Crab Creek Review* and teaches at Bellevue College.

IRA SUKRUNGRUANG is the author of the story collection, *The Melting Season*; two memoirs, *Southside Buddhist* (American Book Award, 2015) and *Talk Thai: the Adventures of Buddhist Boy*; and the poetry collection, *In Thailand It Is Night*. He teaches at the University of South Florida.

EMMA TRELLES is the author of *Tropicalia* (University of Notre Dame Press), winner of the Andres Montoya Poetry Prize and a finalist for Foreword Reviews/Indie Fab Poetry Book of the Year. She is the recipient of an Individual Artist Grant from the Florida Division of Cultural Affairs, and her poems & prose have appeared or are forthcoming in *Political Punch: Contemporary Poems on the Politics of Identity*, *Miramar*, *Poet Lore*, *The Best American Poetry*, *Best of the Net*, *the Miami Herald*, and other places. She lives with her husband in Santa Barbara, California, where she teaches at City College and programs the Mission Poetry Series.

WILLIAM TROWBRIDGE is the author of seven full poetry collections and four chapbooks, most recently *Vanishing Point* (Red Hen Press). His awards include an Academy of American Poets Prize, a Pushcart Prize, a Bread Loaf Writers' Conference scholarship, a Camber Press Poetry Chapbook Award, and fellowships from The MacDowell Colony, Ragdale, Yaddo, and The Anderson Center. A former Poet Laureate of Missouri (2012–2016), he teaches in the University of Nebraska at Omaha low-residency MFA in Writing Program and lives in the Kansas City area.

KERRI WEBSTER is the author of two books of poetry: *Grand & Arsenal*, 2012, and *We Do Not Eat Our Hearts Alone*, 2005. She teaches at Boise State University.

AFAA MICHAEL WEAVER is the author of numerous poetry collections, including: *Spirit Boxing*, *The Plum Flower Dance: Poems 1985 to 2005*; *The Government of Nature*, winner of the Kingsley Tufts Poetry Award; and *City of Eternal Spring*, winner of the Phillis Wheatley Book Award. He is the recipient of an NEA fellowship, a Pew fellowship, four Pushcart Prizes, and a Fulbright scholar appointment, among other honors. In 1998, he became the first Elder of the Cave Canem Foundation. Weaver is alumnae professor of English at Simmons College in Boston.

SHERRAINE PATE WILLIAMS' poems have most recently appeared or are forthcoming in *Southern Poetry Review*, *Measure*, *Zymbol*, *Antiphon*, *Deep South Magazine*, *The Avatar Review*, and *A Bad Penny Review*. A native of Memphis, Tennessee, she now makes her home in Kentucky with her husband and two children. She is an MFA candidate in poetry at Murray State University's creative writing program and currently teaches basic literacy skills to adults.

C. DALE YOUNG is the author of four collections of poetry, the most recent being *The Halo* (Four Way Books, 2016). A recipient of fellowships from the NEA, the Guggenheim Foundation, and the Rockefeller Foundation, he practices medicine full-time and teaches in the Warren Wilson MFA Program for Writers.

IR

INDIANA
REVIEW

Fiction
Poetry
Nonfiction
Artwork

SINCE
1 9 7 6

indianareview.org
inreview@indiana.edu

SUGAR HOUSE REVIEW

AN INDEPENDENT POETRY MAGAZINE

PAST CONTRIBUTORS

Dan Beachy-Quick   Claudia Keelan   Paul Muldoon   Patricia Smith
Anne Caston   William Kloefkorn   Carl Phillips   Janet Sylvester
Kate Greenstreet   Jeffrey McDaniel   Donald Revell   Pimone Triplett
Major Jackson   Campbell McGrath   Natasha Sajé   Joshua Marie Wilkinson

Work from our pages has been included in *Verse Daily, Poetry Daily,* and
Pushcart Prize: Best of the Small Presses, 2015, 2014, 2013, and 2011.

THINK BIG!

VALLUM AWARD FOR POETRY 2017

1st Prize: $750   2nd Prize: $250   + Publication

Mail to:
Vallum Poetry Contest
5038 Sherbrooke West
PO Box 23077 CP Vendome
Montreal, QC H4A 1T0
CANADA

Or Enter Online:
info@vallummag.com (queries only)
www.vallummag.com/contest

JUDGE: Nicole Brossard

Submit a maximum of 3 poems
of up to 60 lines per poem.
Entry Fee: $25 per submission
(includes a 1-year subscription to Vallum)

DEADLINE: July 15, 2017

FIFTH WEDNESDAY
JOURNAL

DEFINING LITERATURE. IN REAL CONTEXT.

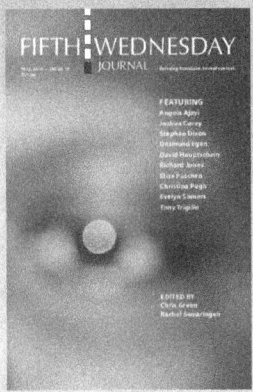

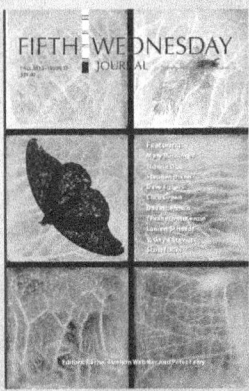
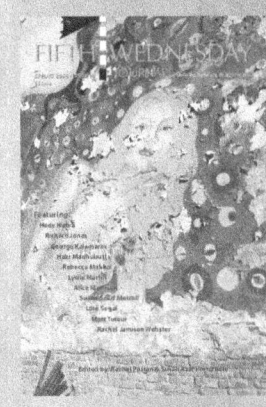

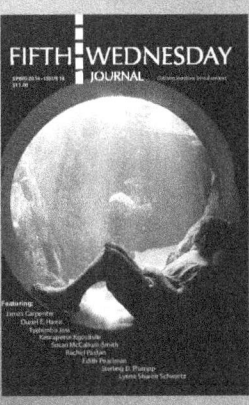

FIFTHWEDNESDAYJOURNAL.ORG

The Carolina Quarterly

POETRY | FICTION | ART | ESSAYS | REVIEWS

www.thecarolinaquarterly.com

www.ingramcontent.com/pod-product-compliance
Lightning Source LLC
Chambersburg PA
CBHW081228020726
47503CB00011B/2941